The publication was effected under the auspices of the Mikhail Prokhorov Foundation TRANSCRIPT Programme to Support Translations of Russian Literature.

Christened With Crosses:
notes taken on my knees
By Eduard Kochergin

First published in Russian as
"Крещенные крестами: записки на коленках"

Translated by Simon Patterson
with Nina Chordas
Edited by Nina Chordas

© Eduard Kochergin 2009
Represented by www.nibbe-wiedling.com

© 2012, Glagoslav Publications, United Kingdom

Glagoslav Publications Ltd
88-90 Hatton Garden
EC1N 8PN London
United Kingdom

www.glagoslav.com

ISBN: 978-1-909156-13-5

Contents

Part 2
WIRE LEADERS

Part 3
CHRISTENED BY CROSSES

FOREWORD

In order to spare my readers vexatious questions regarding the title and subtitle of my tale, I will first explain the second inscription, that is, the subtitle.

First, all events were written down haphazardly, on my knees, in tiny notebooks, in random places, wherever life found me and whenever there chanced to be a rare moment not occupied with the primary work of drawing.

Second, these are notes about a time when the system had the whole country on its knees.

Third, these are the fragmentary remembrances of a kid who got to live to the tune of triumphant marches in a rampant Soviet state orphanage ministry with all its grim claptrap, as did many other young guinea pigs, for a significant number of years.

Notwithstanding, these are simply notes, with no pretensions toward philosophical, sociological, or any other elevated conclusions. These are notes taken on my knees.

"Christened with crosses" is an old expression of former inmates of Russian prisons built on the cruciform plan of the original, infamous Kresty (Crosses) prison in St. Petersburg. It was a term employed by incarcerated denizens of the criminal underworld, whose neighbors during the Stalin years included political prisoners. The expression is capacious and ambiguous.

Bronislava Odynyets
Chita, 1921

To the memory of Mother Bronya,
Bronislava Odynyets

MOTHER BRONYA,
TAKE ME ON AS A SPY

The first conscious memory in my life is linked with the ceiling, Maybe I was ill frequently, or there was some other reason …

I was born out of fear: my father Stepan was arrested for involvement in cybernetics, and my mother gave birth to me two months early.

I liked to lie in bed and travel, looking at the three-layered ornate cornice that decorated the high ceiling in my room. I could look at its fantastic curves for hours, with their strange stems and leaves, and in my mind I would travel along the winding spaces between them, as if through a labyrinth, and if the weather was bad outside, I could hide under the largest of them. At times when it was light, and especially when the sun was shining, I would happily swim over the surface of the ceiling into its center, to the rich baroque rosette, and along the old chandelier with three angels, each of which held three candle-holders with lamps, and I would sink down, tired, back to my bed.

My second memory is linked with baptism and the Catholic Church on Nevsky Prospekt. All of my senses already take part in this memory. That is to say, I don't understand what is happing, but I absorb what is going on. The priest is doing something with me, boys in white are swinging and pouring smoke from shiny metal toys that look like Christmas decorations. There is a lot of white, a great deal of white – clothes, flowers, light. The smell of smoke is unfamiliar and distant, and it seems to me that everyone is in a bit of a hurry, and that there is something unnaturally anxious about all of this. I usually smile a lot, even suspiciously so for my mother Bronya, but I am not smiling.

I also remember the steps that lead to the church. This was my first ordeal in life (after all, I don't remember my father's arrest). For some reason I was forced to walk up them myself – with enormous difficulty, however I could: with my legs, on my knees, with the help of my hands, by rolling up them... I was very young at that time, evidently.

This was the first social entrance in my life, the first theater in my life, the first light in my life, the first music, and the first, still unrecognized love. If this hadn't been in my memory, then my fate would probably have been different.

It was 1939 when I finally started to talk. I started talking in late autumn, and only in Polish. For Mother Bronya was a Pole, and my Russian father was in prison at the Big House. Before that I only smiled when people tried to talk to me, and in general I smiled more than I needed to. I sat there, smeared in everything imaginable, and smiled... And suddenly I started talking, and I said quite a lot. Mother Bronya, of course, was happy, and even organized a Polish meal: with lentils, carrots, and guests.

The next morning they came for her. First the janitor Faina, a Tatar, came into the corridor, and then came a polite military man with a cardboard folder, and someone after him. The polite military man asked her surname and Christian name, and asked several times whether she was Polish, and the others began to rifle through her things, the tables and beds. I tried to tell them that we did not have any bedbugs, but I lisped, and spoke in Polish. Mother asked Faina to call Janek from the first floor, so that he could take me. When Janek arrived, Bronya blessed me with the Mother of God and kissed me. Felya, my elder brother, sat by the window on a chair the whole time and silently rocked back and forth. He was already strange by then.

Faina, the Tatar, took pity on me, a premature child, and gave me to the Poles on the first floor "for safe-keeping". She soon also brought Felya, who was very upset: he hadn't been taken to the Big House, and was told that we were too young to be spies, but would later be sent to some orphanage.

Yes, I was very young. With my Godfather Yanek, a Polish cabinet maker, I travelled under many tables, couches and bunks, and closely studied everything under tables and sundry other "underneaths", and once in one cranny under a table I found something that was hidden from everyone, and was punished for it.

I must say that I liked Yanek's profession of cabinetmaker. I especially liked the wood shavings. They looked wonderful, and smelt delicious. I even tried to eat them.

I also remember Felya, after he was injured from beatings at school for his father being a spy, standing by Janek's large geographical map, running his finger along it and trying to find where our father and Mother Bronya had been taken. Since that time I have always felt a certain hostility towards school. Janek said that our father and mother had been taken to the Big House.

What was this house? And why were spies taken there?

I imagined that in a dense forest with super tall trees, like in the fairytale of "Tom Thumb", the Big House stood, and inside it lived brothers and sisters, who were spies. And what spying was, no one knew except them. This was a big secret. And this was why the forest was dense, and the house was Big. And little kids like me weren't taken there, but I still wanted to go. I was left all alone, as my brother Felya died in a madhouse from pneumonia.

I was sent to a state house, and since that time my life became a part of the state. My ignorance of Russian forced me to keep silent again, as my Polish lisping irritated my class mates, and was dangerous for me: they thought that I was mocking them, and I became dumb again for a long time. We were moved from city to city, from west to east, away from the war, and I ended up in Siberia, near the city of Omsk. All the talking boys around me shouted loudly in Russian and even – so that I would understand – swore, and sometimes fought with me:

"What are you hissing for, snake, speak Russian!"

So I learned Russian, and didn't speak at all until I was four and a half. I agreed with everyone, but didn't say anything, "acting like Mu-Mu", pretending to be a mute[1]. I started speaking Russian unexpectedly even for myself during the war.

---

1 Mute like the deaf-mute master of the dog Mu-Mu in the famous Turgenev story of the same name.

We were fed from mugs – there weren't any plates. There were only metal mugs and spoons. Six people sat at a table – six mugs, and a seventh mug with bread cut into strips that stuck out of it vertically. Soup, then the main course, if there was one, and tea – all from the same mug. And this was considered normal. They let us into the dining hall when all the mugs were on the table, and until then, a horde of hungry boys crowded around the door. The doors were opened, and like animals we rushed to our mugs. Once, a pimpled, sniveling "fly-by", or outsider, was put at our table, and this boy, who ate faster than all of us, unexpectedly licked his dirty finger in front of everyone, and began dipping it in all our mugs. And suddenly I said something loudly in Russian – I didn't understand it myself, but it was something to do with his mother. The dirty boy froze in astonishment, and the rest were afraid: I didn't talk, after all, I was deaf-mute – and suddenly I started talking, and quite impressively. Since then I spoke Russian and gradually forgot my first language.

But I've become distracted from the most important thing, what worried us orphans of the NKVD (People's Commissariat of Internal Affairs) at the time, and the problems that we solved among ourselves:

"Can leaders be people, or do they have to be only leaders, and do they have to have whiskers?"

"Who's better: a spy or an enemy of the people? Or is it all the same? In any event, we're all together here."

When boys met for the first time, they asked:

"Are you a spy?"

"No, I'm an enemy of the people."

"But what if you're both at the same time, like me for example ?"

And also:

"Why is comrade Lenin a grandfather? He didn't have grandchildren, after all. Maybe because he has a beard, or because he's dead?"

"Comrade Stalin is the friend of all children. So that's means he's our friend too?"

Our eldest boy couldn't stand it any longer, and asked the teacher about Stalin. First she got very scared, and then grabbed him by the collar and dragged him to the guard on duty – we heard him crying loudly there. And there were many, many more questions.

I personally believed that spying was not such a bad thing. My Russian father Stepan couldn't have been bad. He was very fine and handsome – look at the photograph. And my dear mother gently sang me lullabies: "Sleep, my darling child, God protect your sleep…", or:

> Z popielnika na Edwasia
> Iskiereczka mruga,
> Chodź! Opowiem ci bajeczkę,
> Bajka będzie długa[2].

O Mother Bronya, take me on as a spy. I'll talk to you in Polish.

---

2   A spark out of the ash-box
    Winks at Eduard.
    Come! I'll tell a story
    The story will be long. (*Polish*)

Part 1
PIPSQUEAK WARD

I'm not Mama's son,
I'm not Papa's son.
I grew on a fir tree,
The wind carried me down…

(Orphan folklore)

THE BALLAD OF THE WOODEN PLANE

I can't remember how I ended up in the orphanage right before the war. My Godfather uncle Janek took me there. Or perhaps I was taken away from him. I don't remember how the war began either. I remember that all of us little mites, as the adults called us, suddenly started playing at war. The other kids made me, who lisped and barely understood Russian, along with two others, a red-headed Tatar and a second large-eyed, black-haired mite – Blackie – into Germans. We were attacked every day, and we surrendered. We were led around the rooms with our hands up, like enemies, and then, shot one by one, we were made to lie on the floor for a long time. I didn't like the game very much.

I remember how the portions of breakfast, lunch and dinner became smaller. And when it got cold and the snow started falling, the kids stopped playing at war.

Then something strange happened. In winter, some enormous Gulliver-like guys came to the orphanage in quilted jackets and earflap hats, and swiftly took away the nine most emaciated boys, four or five-year-old mites. The men had us lined up against the wall, examined us attentively, and ordered the teachers to dress us quickly in the warmest clothes. They hastily put clothes of various sizes on us and gave each of us a heavy woolen blanket. Then, dressed, we went downstairs and out of the building, where a large rumbling bus stood waiting. Two of the guys lifted us up into it in turns. There were a few more adults in the bus in quilted jackets and earflap hats. On the first two seats, seven boys were sat down, and the wall-eyed Snotty and I, the last in line, sat among the guys on the back seat. To my right sat the senior Gulliver. He was in charge of everyone, and everyone obeyed him.

Winter that year was early, snowy and very cold. The entire city was covered in snow. The mounds of snow by the road sides were three times taller than me. None of us knew where the bus was going. When a boy nicknamed Stinky asked where we were being taken, the guy in charge replied:

"To the plane."

"To the plane? That's great! So we'll fly in the air!" we said happily.

"Yes, you'll certainly fly! You'll fly over Lake Ladoga."

We drove through the city for a long time, slowly, without stopping anywhere, even after the sirens howled and the bombing began. It was starting to get dark when we drove out of the city into an enormous snowy expanse, which was crossed only by our road. Suddenly the guys started to get anxious, and the drone of a plane could be heard. The driver increased his speed, we began to be shaken around and thrown from side to side, especially on the back seat. The road turned out to be broken up under the snow. The drone of the plane approached.

"It's a 'Messer'" the driver said. "It's going to follow us."

"Put the children on the floor under the seats right now!" my neighbor ordered, and as soon as we had been pushed under the seats, the bus was riddled with machine gun fire. We probably didn't hear the shots, the motor was humming and growling so loudly that we only realized the Messerschmitt had attacked us by the holes in the roof.

The first attack did not claim any victims. The driver squeezed the last juice out of the motor, to get out of this damn field as quickly as possible. The 'Messer' returned and, at low altitude, it attacked us again. The guy standing by the cabin fell down, and one of the boys screamed horribly… I instinctively looked out from under the seat, and suddenly the 'Messer' moved to the side of the bus and fired a round at the windows on the left side. We were literally showered with a huge amount of glass shards. One of them stuck into my eyebrow above the bridge of my nose. The commander who was sitting next to me immediately lifted me onto his knees and pulled out the shard. Gulping blood, I lost consciousness.

When I came to, I was lying on a bench in some wooden hut. Out of the window, I could see a large white field surrounded by forest. I looked at the world with one eye; my other eye, along with most of my head, was bandaged up.

At that time, I still didn't understand Russian properly. The fur-hatted guy in charge took me from the bench and sat me down next to him, closer to the burning stove, and said something to comfort me. Boys were grouped around the stove, and with serious adult looks they stared at the living flames. After a few minutes, a large copper kettle boiled on the stove, and a little later we were given a metal cup, a sugar cube and a piece of bread. A ferocious fellow with a moustache and beard poured tea into the teapot right out the packet, and stirring the boiling water with an enormous knife, he began pouring a little into our cups. When we had finished our tea, all the Lilliputian boys were told to get dressed, do their buttons up and go into the yard to answer the call of nature. Then each one of us began to be packaged up, wrapped in a wadded cotton state blanket, turning us all into babies stuck into pouches. There were seven of these pouches. Why not nine? Where were the other two boys? – I didn't know how to ask. Perhaps they were seriously injured, or killed when the bus was fired on.

In the darkness, the big guys carried us, like infants, to the plane that was waiting next to the forest. It was quite a large plane, so at the time it seemed to me, and a lot of guys were loading boxes into it, handing them to each other from trucks. The pouches containing us were also put into the plane in the same way, from one pair of hands to the next.

Inside the plane, we were placed in our wadded pouches on wooden benches with backs, attached to the two opposite sides of the plane, and with ropes were firmly tied to them. Between the benches, there was a shooting frame, resembling a stepladder. In the center of four wooden beams that stuck into the ceiling, there was a platform made out of boards with steps. Above it, there was a hole in the ceiling, into which a large machine-gun was fastened. On both sides of this gun there were wooden frames, from the floor to the ceiling and from the right side to the left. Durable boxes were attached to them with ropes. All of the space, apart from the aisles, was filled up with these boxes. This plane had probably been hastily converted from a passenger plane to a cargo plane. The portholes in the form of ovular rectangles were covered with pieces of metal on the inside. The salon was illuminated with two dull flashing lamps. The same guy who had sat next to me on the bus was giving the orders. Everyone else, including the pilots, carried out his orders.

I was bundled up opposite the legs of the shooter, although from below I could only see his enormous black fur boots.

I recall everything that took place in the plane in fragments. Either I lost consciousness from my injury – the shard of glass in the bus had after all hit me hard – or like the other mites, I was given sweet tea with alcohol in it, to stop us from wriggling.

I don't remember our plane taking off. I was probably under the influence of the drink. I woke from the terrible shuddering and severe pitching of the plane, good thing that we had been tied up with ropes, otherwise we would all have slithered across the floor.

How long we flew, I can't say. A weak light was shining through the machine-gun hole – it was probably already getting light. Something was happening to the plane. The guys stood there holding on to the beams of the frames. The shooter was firing his machine-gun from the step-ladder directly opposite me. I didn't immediately realize that he was shooting at the enemies who were following the plane. The pilots, trying to evade attack, began to maneuver in the air, rolling onto the left side of the plane and then the right. At these moments, we dangled from the ropes in the air in our pouches. I don't know how long the unequal battle with the "Messers" lasted. I passed out again. After a while I saw with one eye, as in a dream, that the shooter's step-ladder was being colored swiftly with something dark red. Blood. But where was it pouring from down the ladder, I wondered in my delirium. And suddenly, following the blood, the soldier's body slid down the pine steps onto the floor, his head shattered by a bullet. It began to smell of burning in the plane.

This was the first death that I saw, and I saw it up close. Perhaps because of my injury I didn't really know what was going on. Or perhaps after two and a half months in the blockade, I had already got used to the concept of death. But for some reason I wasn't afraid for myself, or for others. I accepted the soldier's death as a fact. War stupefies people. After the strafing of the bus, and the sight of that blood, something broke off in me – I was stupefied. The only feeling I had was one of cold. My legs in the blanket pouch had turned into frozen drumsticks.

Our wooden plane had evidently been hit. It started burning from the tail. The guys were trying to put out the fire with fire extinguishers. Suddenly a terrible pain pierced my ears – we were descending headlong. I disappeared from the world once more, losing consciousness. I came to when my blanket pouch was torn from the cabin with a savage force. All of the men who had been putting out the fire tumbled to the floor, evidently hit. The plane sliced into the snow-covered bank of a lake, and began sliding across it on its belly. I even remember the strange squeak-hissing sound of the sliding. I remember cries (I didn't understand the words) that the guy in charge made to the pilots from the floor, when the plane braked. After this he got up, crossed himself, as it seemed to me, and started giving orders. He ordered some of his subordinates to quickly remove the pieces of metal from the portholes, break the windows and push us boys through them, and take us fifty meters or so from the plane. He ordered others to save the boxes, pushing them through the windows and doors, and others to put out the fire outside and inside, until the entire plane had been evacuated. He ordered the pilots to remove all the devices, and take the instruments out of the plane, along with the sheets of iron, the dry rations, alcohol and everything valuable they could. The people, like ants before a storm, bustled around the plane, taking boxes, instruments, food and other things out of its belly. I remember that the ropes with which we were tied to the benches were chopped through with axes, and the pouches holding us were pushed through the holes of the windows. I remember that we were all placed on the snow together, in a row.

As soon as the main cargo had been taken out of the burning plane, and dragged away from it as far as possible, the plane exploded. I lost consciousness again for a long time. I came to from the harsh smell of alcohol. In a hut made of boxes and tarpaulin, the adults were rubbing our frozen legs, arms and faces with alcohol. To warm us up inside, they ordered us to drink hot medicine – water with alcohol.

Throughout the day, all the adults built a camp in the snow, resembling a round fortress. In the center of the circle they built a fire, which on the next day was joined by a metal oven assembled by handy men from pieces of iron off the plane. They made spades out of the remains of the metal, and small doors fordugouts. Everything that remained from the plane was used. Around the fire and stove, there appeared five dugouts with walls made of boxes and a floor of fir branches, covered with tarpaulin. I remember that the adults crawled into the dugouts. The warmest dugout belonged to us kids. With each day, our camp improved, and became cozier and warmer. I don't remember how many days we lived in it, but it was quite a long time. Initially we got water from the snow, and then made a hole in Lake Ladoga. To get logs, a road to the forest was cleared in the snow. The guy who was in charge sent the pilots to the nearest villages. They were dressed more warmly and had maps. They had to force their way over ten kilometers through deep snowdrifts.

During the first days we ate the remains of the dry rations, made porridge from rye flour and seasoned it with egg powder. The food was delicious. On the third day, the pilots returned on skis, and brought potatoes, cabbages, carrots, onions and other tasty things on sleds from the village. In honor of them, a feast was organized. We also took part – we were put on benches that the guys cut out of pine trees, and were given a mug of the tea that came from the village. And a whole carrot for each boy, although not all of the boys knew what to do with it.

Not until several days later, two enormous covered vehicles on caterpillar chains came for us. We were packed into the blankets once more, and together with the tied-up boxes, we were put into the all-terrain vehicles. We drove away from the camp as it began to get dark, and we reached a railway station by noon the next day. I remembered that the guys were very careful with the boxes.

Later, at the station, or perhaps in the train, I heard that they contained the blueprints and calculations of our new destroyer plane, and that the guy in charge was the engineer who had created this plane. The engineer was called Sergey, and his surname was Yeroshevsky or Yaroshevsky.

But why did he collect us, state orphans, and not just normal children, in his plane, and take us from blockaded Leningrad? It was strange. Why did this kind Gulliver single me out from all the other Lillputs, and even bandage my head himself? Because I smiled at him with one eye? Or because I was wearing a cross?

We were taken by train to Kuibyshev, and put in the NKVD orphanage. The local teachers took the cross away from me, the only thing that I had left from my mother Bronya.

Part 1

STATE HOUSE

Pictures from remote years, which once seemed ordinary and uninteresting to us, drill themselves into our memory as time goes by, revealing themselves in all kinds of unexpected details.

In the savage times when millions of adults were fighting to the death in the European part of Russia because of two whiskered leaders, far away in Siberia everything was calm. Our life in a model orphanage of the NKVD, hidden in the village of Chernoluchi on the bank of the Irtysh River in remote Siberia, was nothing remarkable. We lived our lives in a state house, as the people said, but in warmth and under the roof of a solid four-story brick building – even if it was a former holding prison, which had become too crowded for adults and was given over for use as an orphanage. The institution became popularly known as the "children's crosses". Traces of feeding troughs remained on the doors of the wards, and prison bars had yet to be removed from some of the windows. But they didn't bother us, on the contrary, and we managed to hide things between the frame and the bars. Our regime was very strict, almost prison-like: wake-up call, exercises, face washing, breakfast, study or work, lunch, sleep, brainwashing, supper, toilet hour, and sleep again – as prescribed by the last person to wear pince-nez in the Soviet Union, the marshal of the NKVD, Lavrenty Pavlovich Beria. But we slept in our own beds with sheets on them, and on Communist holidays and on the birthday of Josef Vissarionovich Stalin – the 21st of December every year – we got without fail a piece of bread with butter on it for breakfast.

Everything was fine and dandy. The children of sentenced parents were called foster-children, and the supervisors were called fosterers. We called the guard "comrade watchman", and the cell was attractively called an isolation ward. Above us all, like a star on a cap, hung the boss, Toad. She was the boss of the bosses: "you can't approach her from behind, and face to face you'll fall over".

Officially, the inhabitants of the orphanage were divided into four levels: the eldest, the older boys, the boys of medium age, and the youngest. The age different between the levels was two to three years. Unofficially, according to the internal situation, the most important older guys called themselves dudes, and the next eldest were called lads. They lived together on the fourth floor and occupied several wards. We, the medium aged, preschoolers from six to eight, were called pipsqueaks, and lived in two wards on the third floor. Opposite us, across the staircase, also in two wards, lived the little kids – under the age of six, in our language called mites. The half of the floor that belonged to them was locked up, and we only saw them in the canteen or in the yard, and through barred windows. On the doors of the wards, our names were scratched: dudes, lads, pipsqueaks, mites.

The left side of the second floor was occupied by the canteen, or as we called it the gobblery or scoffery, and the kitchen. On the right, below us, was the large assembly hall named after Dzerzhinsky, with a portrait of Felix Edmundovich

Dzerzhinsky on the central wall. Below the portrait was a long presidium table, with a red tablecloth on it, and rows of benches by the table. This hall was almost always empty. We were only allowed inside on holidays, when we were made to stand in line during ceremonies and visits by bosses. Behind the wall with the portrait of the goat-bearded Felix, there was another decent-sized room – for meetings of the fosterers and bosses of the orphanage. None of us had been in this room, but we knew that on weekends and holidays, the guards got drunk and celebrated behind the back of their legendary leader. On the side walls of the hall, two enormous paintings hung in frames – "Stalin in the Turukhansky region", and "The Young Leader among the workers of Baku", which the dudes called "Gangsters'Assembly" or "Offloading of Rights".

On the way to the canteen between the first and second floor, on a heavy pedestal that was painted to look like dark red marble, there was a white plaster bust of Grandpa Lenin surrounded by flower pots, which we secretly called "Baldy in the garden". Before Victory Day it was suddenly painted bronze, and the criminal hooligans immediately renamed it "Bronze tank on holiday".

The first floor belonged entirely to the orphanage board and its departments. To the right, by the main entrance to the reception, there was a corridor with the guards' search room, where boys were examined in line after they came back to the orphanage after taking a walk or working. But we adapted to these searches and deftly hid the valuable things we had found outside, by handing them along down the line.

Behind the search room, in a former cell, there was an isolation room and sanitary checkpoint, where new kids were taken – they were kept in quarantine for several days, given treatment and then sent up to the wards.

In the next two wards there was a medical section – one of the most terrifying places in the orphanage, in our language the croakery or kaputka. Few of the children who were taken there returned upstairs. This section was led by a nurse called Absolute Drip. Her assistant, a deaf-mute nursing aide, a dirty animal whose stench killed flies, did not clean up, but simply spread filth around. In summer, the orphans who were doing forced weeding in the shed ate unwashed vegetables out of hunger, and died in Kapa's section from intestinal diseases. Once, after an excess number of children died at the medical section, some commission of officers with epaulets came along and gave the local bosses a dressing down. After they left, we saw the head of the orphanage cursing in foul woman's language and punching Kromeshnitsa's savage eyes with her pudgy fists.

The corridor ended with two cells. They had been prisoners' cells in the preliminary holding area, and remained so, nothing there had changed. In one of the cells, a strange inscription had been scratched on the wall a long time ago: "Some get a tator, others get a lator". Among the pipsqueaks, lads and even the dudes, there were rumors that these cells were haunted by the ghosts of two tormented prisoners of the consignment prison, and that at night they came out onto our staircase, and passing Baldy, also a former prisoner, they went up to the second and third floors. God forbid you should fall into their clutches – they would take you away from this world to the next. We often heard some kind of prolonged groans and strange howls coming from the staircase at night. Perhaps it was just the wind.

OF THE TOAD AND SERVANTS

The second, left half of the lower floor belonged to Toad and her helpers. Don't be surprised, the boss of our orphanage of the NKVD of the USSR was called Toad, and not only by the pupils, enemies of the people, but also by her subordinates, behind her back. This accurate nickname overshadowed her first name and patronymic, and any attempt to remember what her real name was only conjures up an image of an enormous, whiskered woman with short fat arms, many chins and no neck, and small, bulging toad-like eyes, who was always wearing green dresses, silk or wool, depending on the season. There was another memorable quirk that she had – to jump and kick her victim with her two heavy legs, opening her round toad-like eyes enormously wide. Serving in Lavernty Pavlovich's department, she was also an artist – she painted oil paintings. She combined her NKVD qualities with the talent of a great Stalin artist.

Her enormous office, the size of our ward, made up of three rooms, looked like a real artist's workshop. Two large easels, a pedestal with paints and a pitcher with brushes were the main items in the official dwelling of Toad. In the center of the room, between the easels, was a large desk with two chairs by it, and above the boss's "throne" there was a black and white lithographic portrait of the father of all of our institutions, the people's commissar of the NKVD of the USSR, Lavrenty Pavlovich Beria. Directly opposite him, in a gilded frame, was the leader himself, Iosif Vissarionovich Stalin, in a field jacket, with a pipe in his hand, and looking at his fellow countryman Lavrenty with a mysterious smile. Two enormous canvases were on the easels, with the main subject of Toad's entire life as an artist – Stalin and children. Her workshop/office smelt of oil paints, turpentine and aromatic tobacco. She smoked some sort of long cigarettes. Her subordinates gossiped that this was the leader's favorite type of tobacco, and that the boss, as a big shot and his portrait artist, fully deserved them. Her portraits and paintings with the Generalissimo were collected by important military men who arrived at the orphanage in cars.

For all her talent and importance, this lady was disliked at the orphanage by young and old, sisters and brothers, as our dish-washer Mashka Cow Leg said. Even the guards didn't have anything good to say about her. She looked at everyone from on high, as if they were bugs swarming down below which could be crushed at any moment, or sent away into oblivion. Women at these institutions were not distinguished by their love of children or by kindness, women of rank especially.

Toad's right-hand man was the fosterer of the dudes, who was awarded the nickname of Screwface. He was a former senior supervisor sent to us from a colony for minors to strengthen the ranks, or perhaps as punishment for some misdemeanor. He was proud of his origins, and when he recalled his former job, he scratched his hairy hands. Evidently, in the corrective labor colony, he had specialized in using physical force. "Oh, what we gonna do wid him…Oh, we gonna teach him a lesson…" he would say, leading a guilty boy to the cell by the collar.

The closest allies of the supervisor were the three guards – Stump with Fire, Chump with Eyes and simply Cudgel – an old fart, secret officer and chatterbox, who performed the role of driver and expeditor at the orphanage. The first two also worked as key-keepers and light-extinguishers – they put out the lights in the cells before we went to sleep, giving the order to sleep, and locked the doors of the sections that led to the stairwell. According to the dish-washer, who wasn't afraid of anyone, all these guys were cowardly animals who were hiding from the frontline at the NKVD orphanage.

The fosterer of the mites was a stout bag whom the guards called Thunder Thighs. This fosterer woman had no qualms about using colorful expressions. She could say to a kid who got under her feet: "Outta my way, you little castoff, or I'll crush you." The dish-washer Mashka Cow Leg called her a stray tough. And she had even stronger comments on her drinking binges with the guards: "What sort of fosterer is she, for God's sake, she's just a bed with thighs. Securing her own job."

There were another two women who were important for us. One of them was the linen-keeper or head of storage, who gave us clothes, towels, soap, sleeping clothes, bedclothes, and was called

Rusty by the guard for the smallpox scars on her already horrible face. She wore a military uniform, but without epaulettes. An order of the Red Star of Battle with red silk piping was pinned to her faded singlet. There were rumors that she had been a heroic partisan in the Civil War in the Siberian Taiga and got rusty there, i.e. caught smallpox. The partisan barely talked to us, only when the linen was changed, emerging from her basement room with a "Box"[3] cigarette between her teeth, looking over the line of boys with unmoving eyes, and croaking, "Well then, little enemies, you're in line – you want something clean?" Her superiors didn't like her – Rusty, with her medal, was too much of an ideological, fossilized revolutionary. The second woman was the orphanage feeder, the cook who had for some reason turned red permanently, was as fat as Toad, and had the typical nickname of Stewed Pork. The only words that she uttered in our hungry direction when the subject was a second helping was "not allowed", and she would turn her well-fed back to us.

A SEPARATE PARAGRAPH ABOUT FOUR-EYES

Perhaps the only human being among the bosses was the elderly man Yefimych, the book-keeper. If you asked him: "Are you an accountant?", he always replied: "No, I'm a book-keeper." We considered this bald four-eyes to be a strange

---

3 Box and Raketa were the cheapest cigarettes at that time. The people called them nails.

adult: first, he treated us like equals, and second, he smiled when he met us and politely asked: "Well, young man, how is your transverse life?" Of course, none of us could say anything to him in reply, or understand what this "transverse life" was for us pipsqueaks. Many even avoided him. Yefimych wore thick glasses on his memorable large-nosed face. To wipe them, he carried a soft cloth that was attached by a string to the front pocket of a shabby jacket. Every time that he took his misted glasses off, he shut his puffy, red eyes, and always, turning away from everyone, carefully rubbed them with the cloth. The dudes tried to tell us pipsqueaks that when Yefmich rubbed his glasses, he was afraid that thieves would steal the valuable cloth and that he would go blind. This accountant/book-keeper gave the impression of a character from some old unread fairytale.

AUNTIE MASHKA
AND UNCLE THEMIS

There were another two adults who were close and approachable for us. The repair man, as he was officially called, Uncle Themis – Themistocles, a Greek by nationality; and Auntie Mashka, Mashka Cow Leg was her orphanage nickname.

Uncle Themis could do absolutely everything: building, sawing, planing, woodworking, metalworking, soldering, painting, plastering, sharpening and shoe-making. All the verbs of male activity applied to him. Toad exploited him without mercy. He built a bathhouse for her, renovated the stove in the building, made picture frames, stretched canvases, framed them, and made new doors and furniture. In short, he worked like a slave. Day and night, you could see Themis huddled in the barn store room, where the workbench and little hut with a tiny stove were contained; that was where he lived. The NKVD probably sent Themis from his home to Siberia without the right to leave, and gave him over to serfdom at our orphanage. Toad allowed him to take elder boys as helpers for big jobs. This was considered to be a stroke of good fortune, as the craftsman paid them with local homegrown tobacco, in secret of course. And we fools asked him:

"Uncle Themis, are you an Ancient Greek or just a Greek? Thunder Thighs says that you came from the Ancient Greeks."

"That's what makes her Thunder Thighs. I came from the Crimean Greeks."

"Are you a spy or an enemy of the people?"

"I'm not one or the other."

"Why are you here then?"

"Because I'm a Crimean Greek."

"Will they let you go back?"

"I don't know. Ask Thunder Thighs, she knows everything." Auntie Mashka was called Cow Leg because of her inborn disability. On her left leg, instead of a foot she only had a heel – a "hoof". And so she hobbled in an unusual way, in a special shoe. She was famous for her prodigiously foul mouth and a tendency to tipple wine. But there was no kinder person in our entire fenced-off territory. She slipped delicious things to the mites to eat – peeled carrots or young turnips. She doctored the war wounds on their elbows and knees with ribgrass. She also eased the lives of us pipsqueaks, put honey on our bumps or rubbed sunflower oil on our hands if we had burnt them in the oven, always saying to the whippersnapper: "What are you sticking yourself in the oven for, you wanna put out the fire with your hand? She tugged, pulled, scratched, tore and flayed". She defended us from the guards, showering them with such Russian words that they quailed before her, shutting their traps. She did not respect the boss, and if she'd had a bit to drink, she would say of her: "What sort of artist is she – she causes pain and down comes the rain. A toad, in a word." It was thanks to her that our orphanage boss became known as Toad. For these evil words, the latter threatened to sew Mashka's mouth up and throw her out into the street along with her nanny-goat. Of all the orphanage employees, Mashka only acknowledged the workman Themis. He made a pair of boots for her at the end of the war out of pieces of leather he had found somewhere. The left boot was made especially for her hoof. When he had made it, and it fit, Mashka threw a drunken party in the barn, with moonshine. At the end of the party, in her new laced-up boots, she started dancing and singing obscene ditties, one of which I remembered all my life:

> Out of the forest dark and thick
> Twelve elephants hauled an enormous dick.
> Sprawled across their backs it lay
> All chained up, and on display.

You couldn't create a more monumental image than this. It's simply the Stalinist Homer.

MASHKA, NYUSHKA AND PENCILS

Mashka Cow Leg had a helper – the young Nyushka, or as she was called at the orphanage, "Little Nyurka, tender belly". She was a fat but still green girl, with small darting eyes in the pink softness of her face. Watching the languid walk of the "tender belly" with a cunning eye, Auntie Mashka for some reason addressed me, a pipsqueak, saying: "Look, Nyushka's flouncing around, looking for a tool, and as our Bolsheviks say, 'he who seeks will always find.' "I didn't understand everything back then, although I had already realized a lot of things.

The duties of these women included various feats: tidying and cleaning the cells (excuse me, wards), corridors, staircases, toilets, slop pails, the isolation cell, and washing the dishes... Auntie Mashka, because of the thinness of her legs, and as she said, "a hard life in the trouser fly of the Bolsheviks", was responsible for washing the dishes, and the young Nyurka, with our help, took care of everything else, not without pride showing off her bare thighs. The guards stared at her carnivorously and would have got their hands on her long ago, if it hadn't been for Cow Leg. The washing of the staircase was called "Nyushka's cinema". Out of all the corners, our older boys ran downstairs, grabbing their things, until they were sent away by the watchmen or Mashka came along.

Part 1

Sometimes we were taken for educational purposes to some factory. This visit outside was the only amusement for everyone, but we also waited for it impatiently because "a hungry thief is fed by the road" – you could get something for yourself if you looked.

I didn't even recognize my first theft, I didn't notice it. We boys were taken to some office; I don't remember what was there, and what we did. All I remember is a picture: opposite the window, with his back to me, a tall man was bending over, almost lying on the table, writing or drawing something on a huge sheet of white paper. To his right there was a box of finely sharpened colored pencils. This was the first time I had seen colored pencils since my brief childhood. And I don't remember how the box ended up under my state-issued jacket. It was mine, it belonged to me and only me. I carried the valuable item under my arm and thought about nothing else but how to keep the only thing that was mine.

In the ward, I managed to shove the box unnoticed between the sheet and mattress. During supper, I was constantly afraid that someone would swipe my treasure. At night, when all the boys were snoring, I tore the seam of the mattress with a razor blade and put the pencils inside it. All I had to do was get a thread and sew up the hole with a "thief's seam", so that any moment, pulling on the knot, I could quickly open up the mattress.

Everything was going well. By evening the next day I already had a thread, and in the morning, during breakfast, I planned to carry out this operation in the empty ward. But this time, life did not smile on me.

In the morning, after wake-up, the guards came with the teachers, lined up all the boys in their underwear in the large space between the beds, and carried out a search under the leadership of the senior watchman, nicknamed Fiery Hyena, who was experienced in these matters. He was the one who shook the pencils out of my mattress.

I was thrown into the cell – after being worked over first, of course. At that time, you must understand, it didn't take much. After the second blow I crossed myself and lost consciousness. Crossing myself stopped the giant watchmen from further violence, something stirred inside them. I was taken to the isolation cell and thrown on a dirty sack filled with hay.

I came to in the arms of Auntie Mashka. With a soft, wet rag, she carefully rubbed my face, and in filthy language damned all the local "generals" and "generalesses":

"Ooh, damn vermin…rotten swine… servile souls… fighting little kids instead of the Germans! The Devil's spawn doesn't even touch little kids, it fears God, but who the hell are you? What shell did you hatch from, what beast conceived you?! Deserters, dogfaces! You stuff your gobs on kids' rations and go nuts from inactivity… you should make a poster: 'beating up kids isn't killing Germans' – and go on and sit under it, and fart into a rag, you government hounds… And these fosterers, – God forgive me, no one stops them – and so they lord it over you destitutes. Better they should drink a little red wine instead of human blood, jackals of the pharaoh…"

"You curse quite insultingly, Cow's Leg. Aren't you afraid that with all this cursing, you'll fall down and won't get up again?" the old guard said.

"Shut up snake! You old birdbrain, you've sucked everything suckable from all the bosses, and you should retire, you evil spirit, to pray for your sins and repent – you earned your fiery hyena reputation a long time ago… Am I afraid? You damned wretches! If anyone gets scared of you, it'll go to your heads. You yourselves were born in fear, you live in fright, and you'll die slaves, you thrice-cursed skunks… Where can I fall? I sit low and look up from the bottom, and if you're thinking of ratting on me, I'll drag you with me to prison, and I know how, you taught me yourselves. You went bitch yourselves and turned everyone else into bitches…"

"That's enough from you, shut up, Mashka, it's hard enough as it is, and your kid will recover and get a stronger head for it. Come and drink with us!" the Fiery Hyena begged.

I asked Auntie Mashka, when she brought me food:

"Why is there a blue cross on the door of the isolation cell, and not a red one?"

"The devil knows… maybe he painted it there. Seems the color red is not for him – he's not of the Soviet persuasion. And you're not put here to be treated, but to turn blue from various torments. If the cross was red, you'd have to be treated."

I dreamt of the pencils constantly, until when I was free, in Petersburg, many years later Mother Bronya bought me some after serving her sentence for "spying", with the pennies she earned by washing floors.

To talk about the other people, who did not have much importance for us, would simply be a waste of time. There were all kinds of them, but they weren't interesting enough to remain fixed in my memory.

ABOUT THE BATH-HOUSE

Right on the edge of the village, across the road, on the bank of the Irtysh River, the second half of the orphanage was located – the female, or girls' orphanage, where little enemies were held in a three-story brick building, the daughters of enemies of the people and spies. On this territory, in a separate structure with a large chimney, a bath house was located, where we were marched in order under the command of Toad's underlings once a week to wash. We had never actually seen the girl enemies. They were not allowed into the yard during our visits. But when we returned past their house, steamed and with dirty clothes under our arms, from their dark windows on all three floors, we were watched by the many curious eyes of our underage partners in crime.

ABOUT MYSELF AND TOYS

Each of the shaven-headed children at the orphanage had their own personal qualities, but did not show them in communal life. We pipsqueaks were allowed as much as was considered proper, i.e. as much as an older boy or stronger ward mate allowed us. We only called each other by the nicknames that we gave to each other, sometimes forgetting the real names of our room-mates.

I tried not to get involved in any disputes or fights. If possible, I even tried to disappear at the sign of any trouble. Gradually, I became good at this – I vanished like a shadow, imperceptibly, and it helped that I was terribly skinny – I crept along the wall. This is how I got the nicknames of Shadow and Invisible Man. If I had any abilities back then, it was in disappearing. I was good at vanishing when necessary, or simply when I wanted to. The guards were amazed: there I was – and suddenly I was gone, out of their clutches.

Once, in a town on the way to Siberia, we orphans were taken to a hospital to be examined by doctors. We walked past a house with a porch to get there. The large ornate door was open for some reason. I suddenly felt myself drawn toward it, and I did not resist. Without being noticed, I detached myself from the group, and found myself in a dark, wide entrance room. More doors appeared, to the left, to the right and in front of me. I chose the right door. I slowly opened it and entered a large room illuminated by three windows, with a beautiful porcelain stove. The room was almost empty. Besides the small couch and two antique chairs, on the clean parquet floor I saw a solid wooden chest – a box with strips of metal around it, with an open lid, and scattered around it were many amazing children's toys. It was quite a wonder for me. I couldn't even imagine that there could be so many toys in the world.

My mother, who lost her job when my father was arrested, lived off day-work. She had no money to buy me toys. I grew up without them, and so I turned everything around me into a playing area. In short, I played at everything and with absolutely everything: with shadows on the wall or the ceiling, with sun rays, with any crawling or flying insects – flies, bugs, ants. With the wallpaper patterns, finding in the combinations of lines the heads of various monsters and beasts which Mother Bronya had told me about. From the stains on the ceilings or the marks from leaks on the walls, I created terrifying monsters, crocodiles, *carcadiles*, as I called them at the time, or even worse, fierce, mysterious hippopotamuses, which I am still afraid of. And if I got hold of something substantial, that I could work with, then I forgot myself, I was happy – I created, trying to make something of my own. The object I found ended up being unscrewed, broken or torn, and my mother, coming home from her hard day at work, would find me on the bed, always dirty, among the remains of some random object, but always smiling. For a while she was even worried that I was not quite right in the head. Another memory from that pre-war time, connected with toys, has remained fixed in the memory of my eyes. The aunties on my father's side, when they learned that I had become an orphan after my mother's arrest, came to Leningrad from their Old Believers' North, with the aim of baptizing the boy in the ancient faith of the Pomorye belief, so that their angels would protect him in captivity. They persuaded my godfather Janek to give them their nephew for the day for family reasons, and secretly took me away on a red tram, far, far away, across the entire city, to the Znamensky Church in the village of Rybatskoe. They didn't know that Mother Bronya had already baptized me as a Catholic. At one stop, from out of the window of the tram, I saw many brightly-colored toys in a shop window. Planes, tanks, cars, elephants, horses, teddy bears, dollhouses, bouncy balls and other things that I did not recognize but found very interesting filled the entire shop window from top to bottom. I glued my face to the glass, greedily watching this display, but the tram moved on, and everything that had just appeared before me drifted past my eyes, turning into an unreal dream. My stern Russian aunties pulled me away from the glass with difficulty, but the vision remained in my memory all my life.

As we entered the dark church, the Aunties whispered for a long time in their Pomorye dialect with an old man wrapped in an enormous beard. Then the old man put on a gown and straightened his beard, and turned into a priest, and led me to a large metal dome filled with water. He made me get up on a stool, and feeling my resistance pinched me painfully on the bottom, then holding me by my curls, abruptly dipped my head into the water. I cried out from surprise and pain.

"He hollered out loudly – he's calling his Guardian Angel. Patience, boy, you are entering life. Life is pain, and you must get used to it," the old Pomorye priest spoke a message to me through the darkness.

Then, singing some chants, he led us around the dome several times, performed some other actions, told us to kiss the eight-ended cross, and finally let us ago.

We returned in the dark. I did not see the shop window with the toys in it on the way back, and when I got to the orphanage, I forgot this wonder, until I happened to enter a boss's house with piles of toys left over from before the war. Among their endless diversity, my eye was caught by a train with a black engine on red wheels, with green wagons and three platforms. Cannons stood on two of them, and there was a tank on the third. To start with I was simply speechless from amazement, I was taken aback from the unexpectedness and accessibility of what I saw to such an extent that I did not immediately notice, among all of these amazing toys, that there was a boy in a fancy shirt and short pants, sitting on a painted wooden horse among the little houses, boats, trains, cars, bears, cats and other treasures. The boy was my age, but domestic and well groomed. When he saw me, a dystrophic child, he froze for a moment and blinked his bright capricious eyes in my direction. Sensing my hungry interest in his possessions, he jumped off the horse and started gathering up the toys from the floor in his pink hands, showing them from all sides and taking them away, putting them in the chest, mocking me with his property. I felt a great dislike for his greediness, and I subconsciously committed a sin before my guardian angels. When the boy, having picked up a red fire engine from the floor, was putting it into his chest, leaning over the edge, I lifted his fat buttocks up into the air, helping him tumble over into the toy chest. The lid of the chest shut of its own accord, the catch of the lock clicked shut, and the boy was trapped. He screamed loudly in the closed chest, and I instantly disappeared, without taking a single toy out of his fairytale. At that time I wasn't stealing yet, but only looked at things.

ORPHANAGE GAMES

Our games and amusements at the orphanage differed considerably from normal children's games. We had nothing, and any rubbish that we happened to find in the yard or on the street when we went to the bath house or somewhere else became extremely valuable. We picked up everything: buttons, pieces of wire, bent old nails, washers, screws, bolts, pipes, bobbins, discarded blades from safety razors, pieces of cardboard and paper. We collected everything we could, just in case. We hid what we collected in secret places in the yard and the wards. Then we invented some "dream" toy made of these random objects, and played with the things we had made. For example, the elder boys made their favorite mayalka[4] out of goat hide and lead from discarded batteries. Only the dudes played this game, and in private – between the stacks of logs in the courtyard, putting us pipsqueaks on watch. They played for food – breakfasts or suppers.

Almost each one of us had a slingshot. The rubber bands for them were pulled out of underpants or trousers. We hunted crows, which were quite numerous in the area. The shooter who killed the most crows was given the title of crow prince or marshal. We made the pellets for shooting out of metal wire.

In 1944, we started to receive American aid. I can't say what went directly to us wards of the state,

---

4 A piece of goat hide pressed between two lead or copper disks so that the fur stuck out of the edges. The diameter of the mayalka was 5-6 cm. They played with the mayalka by kicking it in the air, counting the number of kicks.

probably macaroni. We had no idea what this was before that year. We filched the cardboard boxes that contained the American food product from the yard, unfolded them and used them in many of the things we made. For example, we made excellent checker pieces from this thick cardboard. The pieces of cardboard, cut out in the right size, were glued together carefully, sanded down and painted black. The pattern was made with a stencil. When it had all dried out, we covered it with spirit varnish. The varnish meant that the cardboard checkers became hard, and when they landed on the table they made a clinking noise, like real ones. The checkers were made with the guidance and help of the "ancient Greek", Uncle Themis. He boiled glue for us, and gave us sandpaper and varnish. Over time, the quality of the checkers reached such perfection that the guards took two sets from us for themselves.

Later, for Victory Day, the older boys made three "fighting" explosives, and to the noise of the official salute in honor of the victory over fascist Germany, they held a "firework" display. One of the boys was injured – the sulphur from the matches burnt his fingers.

The most forbidden game at the orphanage was cards. The kids played 21 or 31, I don't remember any other games. Of course, the elder boys were the ones who played. We, as always, stood guard. The cards were also made at the orphanage. This was considered to be a skilled job, and not everyone could do it. Certain skills were required. While I was still an ordinary pipsqueak, I began to try my hand at drawing cards. I was not strong or tough. The mocking chants about me, "skeleton of seven years, head on a stick", were quite accurate. And the need to defend myself from beating and humiliation in some way forced me to start making "flowers", or playing cards; by doing this I could save myself. Over time, as I mastered the craft, I won out over others who wanted to do this respectable work, and spent entire days producing them. In five or six days I would make an entire deck, and give it to the players. Everyone liked my cards, and the dude in charge began to keep watch over me, that is, no one could touch me.

At the orphanage, I realized intuitively, and then with my head, a simple truth – in the gang, good craftsmanship was valued.

In the summer of 1945, I was promoted from pipsqueak to lad for my talents, and that was already the path to becoming a dude.

ON COCKROACHES

Of all the deeds that the dudes entrusted to us pipsqueaks, the most interesting was catching cockroaches. The fact was that from time to time, the elders blew them into the crack between the door and the floor, into the office of the hated boss Toad. This partisan operation was considered to be extremely dangerous, and all the initiated specially prepared to carry it out. Our pipsqueak duty was to supply live cockroaches to the dudes, and we tried our utmost. During wartime, catching German cockroaches was an ideological activity for us, we did not capture cockroaches, but fascists, so our enthusiasm was constant. There were plenty of the whiskered bugs in the orphanage, especially around the kitchen and canteen. Hiding from the guards, we would drive them into special traps that we made out of pieces of newspaper, catch them with our hands, lure them with breadcrumbs into matchboxes, bottles and so on. When we had filled several paper traps or matchboxes, we gave them to the dudes. They put the cockroaches into tubes specially rolled up out of pieces of paper, with a thick, twisted end, and blocked the other end with a cork made of twigs or paper – and the missile was ready. They would collect a few of these and wait for a convenient moment to attack.

Usually, the partisan attack took place on Sunday or on Red holidays, when Toad was not in the orphanage, and our guards were getting drunk. The dudes crept in turn to the door of the boss's office, slipped the twisted end of the paper pipe into the gap between the floor and the door, pulled the cork out of the other end, and lying on the floor, they blew hard into the tube. The twisted end became untwisted, and the cockroaches flew into the office. In summer, during walks, they blew cockroaches from the yard into the open window using a tubular plant that was known as an "umbrella" in Siberia. With these natural pipes, we also made pumps and poured water over each other, distracting the Cerberus-guards' attention from the military operations.

Toad couldn't understand how the damned cockroaches got into her office/workshop, and in such huge numbers. Among the young pipsqueaks and mites, someone spread the legend that the bosses ate the cockroaches with a special sauce. One of the boys even asked the Fiery Hyena – the guard by the outside door: was it true that he ate cockroaches with sauce? For which he got a hefty blow on the head.

PIPSQUEAK WARD

Our pipsqueak existence unfolded, as I said before, in two wards on the third floor. In one small ward, made of two cells of the former jail, the younger pipsqueaks, the Mensheviks, were held, and in the larger ward of three cells, we lived, the Bolsheviks. As was proper, we oppressed the Mensheviks according to the law of seniority.

The remains of brick walls between the former cells divided the large ward into three. The three barred windows were opposite three doorways; in two doorways where the doors were firmly sealed, there were small tables for exercises and games, and in the third doorway there was a functioning door.

If the youngest had to obey us, in our turn we unfailingly obeyed the lads and the dudes, which meant that we had to kowtow to them according to the local rules. And there was no complaining, otherwise you'd get a blow to your shaven head, or a "bicycle" at night – you'd get your toes burnt in your sleep.

In our ward, we rarely argued and hardly ever fought. The pipsqueak authority selected by the dudes, the strongest among us, was a boy with the surname Rotov, Rot or Mouth for short, while his full nickname was Nosey Crookedmouth. He was not known to behave like a beast, and did not bother the other boys. Among the other numerous pipsqueaks, Pete Bronze Horseman stood out – he got this name from the boss Toad for sitting on Mashka's fierce goat in the yard of the orphanage. He was a constantly hungry glutton, and Mashka said of him that he looked with his mouth and thought with his stomach. Then there was a red-haired boy who liked standing watch, with the nickname Bedbug, whom everyone so inclined chased in the yard during walks, with cries of "Squash him!" After him came Bebeshka[5], the only one among us who played mayalka, and constantly forfeited his breakfast to the dudes. And of course, Lumpy Aerodrome, a wide, neckless boy with a flat aerodrome-shaped head, on which everyone who walked past him landed a click of the fingers. He squatted down to reduce the blow of the clicks from the strong dudes, and blinked his goggle eyes.

I would especially like to mention Dumkin Wetty – a completely helpless kid. He lived on the very edge of the room, by the door, because he wet himself every day. Despite his great oddities, for some reason we felt sorry for Dumkin. Every day, an hour before bed, and sometimes in the mornings, he marched in the central space between the beds, chanting a silly song: "Kyr-pyr, eight holes, kyr-pyr, eight holes". Once the head supervisor Screwface, hearing the chant of "kyr-pyr" and seizing our Dumkin by the collar, turned him to face himself and started looking him over like a rabbit sentenced to the slaughter, with his cold, glassy python eyes. And shaking Wetty, he asked:

---

5   Bebeshka – one of the names for the mayalka game.

"Do you know what kyr-pyr is? Eh?"

"No..."

"Who taught you this then? Eh?..."

"I don't kno-o-o-w," he whimpered.

"Kyr-pyr is an abbreviation of 'red proletariat', and your chant is slander of the proletariat and the Soviet regime. Come with me, little rat!" And lifting him by the collar of his jacket, he dragged the terrified Dumkin to the cell. He was held there on starvation rations, and interrogated every day, until he went silent.

Several days later, Wetty appeared in the ward, skinny and quiet. He didn't march between the beds anymore. He only asked everyone who entered the room in a weak voice: "Where have you been, what did you eat?" Once he asked this question of an important official in epaulettes, who came to us on an inspection:

"Where have you been, what did you eat?"

All of Toad's minions accompanying the officials yelped in fear that the pupil was disturbed, and needed treatment. The official stood before the frozen Wetty, looked at him thoughtfully, and then turning to Toad, ordered:

"Treat him immediately."

The next day, Dumkin disappeared from our pipsqueak life forever. The tender-hearted Auntie Mashka told the stinking supervisors that they had taken sin upon their breasts before their Marxes and Engelses. It was wrong to hurt Dumkin, he was protected by God.

The night-time pipsqueak life for us began after the departure of the last Cerberus-darkener,

Blockhead with Eyes, who put the lights out in the room before bedtime. Blockhead turned off the light switch, i.e. put the light out in the rooms, ordered us to go to sleep in his drink-sodden voice, and hung a solid warehouse padlock on the door of the pipsqueak section, from the stairwell side. After his keys had stopped jingling, an amnesty was announced in the room, and we began to live our own lives. The pipsqueaks did their most forbidden and sacred things at night. If the moon was shining out the window, then we got working materials and tools from their secret places. Everyone who could use their hands made something worthwhile, necessary, including fighting slingshots and pellets for them. At the same time, one of us would tell various terrifying stories or real-life incidents. Recollections of food from the times of freedom were popular – who ate what before the state house. Personally, during the amnesty I worked on playing cards, or made profiles of leaders by bending copper wire. We went to sleep two hours after lights out.

THE VICTORY PAINTING

The main working obligations of the pupils were connected with the yard and the kitchen. We swept the yard, tidied the paths, in autumn we gathered up leaves in piles and burnt them, in winter we shoveled the snow and tidied the paths once more for walks. Under the leadership of Themis, we gathered piles of wood for the winter; the firewood was split by prisoners. At the end of winter, we sorted vegetables in the basements, mainly potatoes. In the summer, the older boys among us were taken to weed carrots, beetroots and turnips in the fields of the NKVD farms. We worked next to adult prisoners, but they weren't allowed near us.

The most difficult duty was considered to be posing for the Stalin paintings of the artist Toad. She painted her children using us as models – the sons and daughters of enemies of the people and spies.

I especially remember the spring of 1945. For the painting "Children congratulate Comrade Stalin on Victory", Toad selected several children from among us pipsqueaks, including me. According to her conception, the congratulation ceremony took place in an apple orchard. We were taken one at a time, or sometimes two at a time, into the garden that grew behind the house where she lived with an old auntie, Wrinkly, and two roosters. We never saw any chickens.

Right after breakfast, directly from the canteen, the orphanage guide Chatterbox would take me with him to the place of torture. On the way he constantly made moralizing speeches, distracting my attention from the search for valuable things that could be found for our inventions. In the orchard, under his observation, I swapped my state uniform for a white shirt and short pants, instead of shoe covers I put on new sandals, and receiving a bouquet of field flowers in my hands, in my new disguise I stood under the blossoming apple tree to wait for Toad to appear. Meanwhile, Chatterbox carried out of the house a folding easel, a canvas on a frame, and a box on legs with paints in it. He slowly arranged the items opposite me, and only then did he go to get the artist. Two minutes later, a long cigarette between her teeth, Toad floated out the door of the house. Without saying hello, she went right up to me, with her fat paws turned my head into the position she required, raised my hands with the bouquet above my shoulders, and ordering me not to move, she began her work. The hardest thing about this job was to keep still under the attack of malevolent spring mosquitoes, which were trying to eat me whole. If I tried to shoo them away, Toad would leap over to me with a hiss, and pinching me painfully, would put my joints in place. I returned to the orphanage all swollen from the mosquito bites, and with a heavy head from Chatterbox's lectures. One day later, I was taken back to Toad's garden to feed the fierce insects.

I saw the finished painting in summer in the office/workshop, where I was summoned by the boss after someone had informed on me for also making art – profiles of Iosif Vissarionovich Stalin and Vladimir Ilich Lenin out of copper wire, and right in front of everyone's eyes.

As I entered the office, I recognized myself portrayed on the canvas, quite a good resemblance, only well-fed, pink-cheeked, with an ingratiating little face, holding out a bouquet of flowers to the leader. Against the background of the blossoming apples trees, among the cheerful retinue of children, the leader and teacher stood, in a white marshal's jacket with the order of Victory. I, the smallest, was raising my head to gaze with my devoted eyes at the white generalissimo god – the conqueror of fascists. I was initially struck dumb by the canvas I saw, but then even exclaimed: "That's wonderful!" Then I imagined that I was being overcome by mosquitoes again, and I started itching as I stood before the painting. Toad interrupted my withdrawal, and snorted:

"Well then, you mangy little kid, show me your trick with the profile of Stalin."

Silently, I took out a coil of copper wire from the pocket of my pants, straightened it out, stretched it until it was of an ideal smoothness, and started bending it, gradually creating a profile, starting with the neck and chin, from the bottom up, in a circle. Toad watched my hands very attentively, and when I finished the head and started on the neck from the other side, cutting off the remains of the wire, like on award medals, she took the long-sighted spectacles off her face and asked me to put the profile of the leader on the table. I carried out her order, and lay the wire Stalin in front of her. Peering at it with her goggling toad's eyes, she snapped:

"Clever! But don't you dare ever to do that again, or you'll be thrown in the special cell, or worse. It's not appropriate to make leaders out of wire. Remember that all your life."

It seemed to me that she uttered these last words with a certain fear, not for me of course, but for herself. As I left Toad's office, I looked at her painting once more – a robust cockroach was taking a tour of it.

After the interrogation, back in the room, I realized that I had been wrong to show her my skills, and that I should have pretended to be a fool, and said that yes, I had tried, but it didn't work out. Indeed, she soon started picking on me. Stump with Fire, on her orders, searched me twice a week, and took everything that he found in my pockets or in the table. And earlier, on 9 May, she shut me in the cell, when I was ill, for coughing during a ceremonial assembly in the yard of the orphanage in honor of the Victory over fascist Germany. And there was nothing I could do but to prepare to flee from this OMSK[6] to my home, which is what I eventually did, but somewhat later.

WHAT WE SCOFFED, GOBBLED AND GUZZLED

Food was the main topic of our life. The dreams of the orphans mainly revolved around food, especially in winter and spring. During that time, as our hobbling lady said, we were liable to eat everything that wasn't nailed down. In summer we ate weeds, risking catching a colon infection and falling into the clutches of the Absolute Drip.

We were fed in the large communal canteen, which we called the scoffery, on the second floor. Six boys sat at each rectangular table. Around the perimeter, there were six green metal mugs, and a seventh in the center, with pieces of rye bread sticking out of it in vertical strips – six pieces. Six soup spoons lay between the mugs, and that was it – there weren't any plates, we ate the first, second and third course from the mugs. The menu was not distinguished by its diversity. We gobbled three types of soup – pea, cabbage and groats; the groat soup with pickled cucumbers was called brine. For the second course, we were usually given some

---

6 OMSK – Remote place of exiled prisoners

porridge – millet or barely, more rarely potatoes, and potatoes with cabbage, under the name of vegetables. The second course was thoroughly scraped out of the mugs, to clean them for the sweetened pale pink jelly or stewed fruit drink, with no fruit in it – this was our main delicacy. We also had porridge for breakfast and supper. Barley groats in the morning, wheat in the evening, or the other way around. Rarely, we were given pea porridge – delicious grub. From 1944, on weekends we were sometimes fed milk soup, with the macaroni that we had not known about until this year.

On holidays – the 1st of May, the 7th of November, the 5th of December, on the Day of the Stalinist Constitution, and on the 21st of December, the leader's birthday, we were given a piece of bread withcream butter, and instead of jelly we got boiled milk in our cups, and for supper, we were given a real sugar lump each in our soup spoon. This was the song. It would all have been fine, but the rations were so tiny that we were half-starved when we got up from the table.

A small person who craved to eat something delicious and voiced this out loud was mocked by the pipsqueaks: "Maybe you'd like cocoa with cream and a bun with marzipan?" No one knew what cocoa was, and we couldn't imagine a bun with marzipan. Where this fantasy came from, especially in that time of hunger, is unclear. Probably one of the adults had said what he dreamed of aloud, and it turned into a teasing chant for us.

I made my first acquaintance with marzipan fifty years later, and in Paris. It was nothing special.

ON ICECREAM
AND YEPTON, THE GOD OF WINTER

In 1944, the air began to smell of Victory. Vague hopes for better times appeared, yet hopes nevertheless. Even at our orphanage! In autumn, at one of the night amnesties, it was decided to celebrate the New Year of 1945 with ice cream. Yes, ice cream, made by pooling the resources of all the pipsqueaks in our ward. None of us really knew for certain what ice cream was. The elder pipsqueaks vaguely recalled that it was milky, cold, sweet and filling, and if it was filling, then it had to have bread in it. From the beginning of winter, we decided to gather the ingredients that made up our dream. From three holidays – the November holidays, the Day of Stalin's Constitution and his birthday – we accumulated a supply of sugar. It was easier for us to get bread, for a few days we divided five pieces of bread at breakfast, lunch and dinner into six pieces, and put one in the hiding place. Getting milk was more complicated. It was given to us at lunch on the 21st of December. By that day, we had filched a couple of empty vodka bottles from the guards, washed them, and under the tables we filled the bottles with milk, the main item on the New Year menu. Since the frozen treat was called ice *cream*, we had to gather a certain amount of creamy butter. We were only given it on holidays, like the sugar, but to make sure that the pupils didn't steal from each other, the butter was smeared on a piece of bread. We moved it to the edge, to the crust of the bread, with our teeth, and took the crust to our room.

The milk and butter that we got this way we hid between the two frames in the window that was the furthest from the entrance. One of the frames especially opened together with the strips of paper that were glued to it during winter. No one could have thought that the hiding place of Father Yepton was behind it. We didn't know anything about Santa Claus, we pipsqueak orphans, but about Father Yepton, the Siberian God of Frost, who healed some and crippled others – our life teacher Auntie Mashka had told us a lot of stories. In her stories, the god Yepton ate nothing but frozen food.

In the night of the 30th-31st of December, on the last room amnesty of 1944, all the pipsqueaks made ice cream. The bread, cut into small squares, was soaked in milk in two bowls, which we had borrowed from Auntie Mashka. Then we poured ground sugar all over the soaked bread pieces, and carefully laid them on boards from the bottom of our bedside table drawers. We placed these trays with the bread between the frames into the Yepton cooler, to freeze. About twenty minutes later, we again soaked the frozen pieces in milk and poured sugar over them, and we did this three times, and four. Before the last freezing, we smeared butter on one side of the pieces – and the product was ready. We worked in shifts, as we were freezing – a minus 30-degree Yepton was raging outside. We poured the finished ice cream into a sack made out of a singlet. Until New Year's Eve we kept the sack of ice cream in the same place – between the windows, covering it from prying eyes with a piece of paper. We were afraid that the guards would find it, but it all went fine! They didn't care about us – they were preparing to celebrate New Year themselves.

On the 31st, as if to order, the God of Winter gave us a clear moonlit night. It was as bright as daylight in our ward. In the central space, we contrived a "tribal" table" out of five bedside tables. We took the precious sack out of the secret window, and counted out for each boy his share of the rye novelty. After the New Year amnesty was announced by the master of the chamber, Crookedmouth, we began to devour the home-made ice-cream of our pipsqueak group – in honor of 1945 and in honor of the Siberian God of Frost, Father Yepton. Not before or after, never again in our lives, have any of us eaten such delicious rye ice-cream – in the light of an enormous moon in a white frozen oriole outside the window.

On the 1st of January we wished Auntie Mashka a Happy New Year and gave her several portions of our ice cream. As she looked at the present, the greatest curser of the orphanage suddenly said, for the first time in our memory:

"Oh Lord, Mother of God! My dear little ones…" And she started to cry.

FESTIVE FRINGE

At the beginning of the year 1945, the orphanage began to prepare for the Victory celebrations. In February, several women were brought in from a women's prison or colony, under guard. In the hall of Felix Edmundovich, we were lined up in front of them, from the mites to the dudes. The prisoners picked different sized boys and took their measurements. After the measuring women had left, there was talk on the floors that we would have a new uniform sewn for us by spring.

The last time the orphanage gang had its hair cut was in February. In April, a rumor spread around the rooms that for the next haircut, in honor of Victory we would have our fringes kept. Initially, none of us believed this nonsense. We thought that as always, we were being taken in. On 20 April, it was announced that on the next day, that is the 21st, the orphans would have their hair cut. 21 is a lucky number in the criminal world – so this meant that our fringes would be kept.

On the morning of the 21st, guarded by armed soldiers, four prison barbers were brought in. We were taken to the hall by floors, starting from the youngest, as usual. The first mites to come away from Dzerzhinsky had their fringes left on. So that meant we would have our fringes kept, we had triumphed, soon peace time would begin and we would all return home!

In the hall, we found that by Toad's demand, the fringes were supposed to be identical, and that we would have our hair cut by a stencil. Each boy, when his turn came, had to hold on his head with both hands a stencil cut out of thick paper, and the haircutter removed all the hair around it with a hand-held hair shaver. The job was tidied up by another prisoner, with scissors. The line consisted of two prisoners with shavers and two with scissors, stencils and our heads. The hairdresser prisoners worked all day until late in the evening, without stopping. In the night of the 21st-22nd of April, for the first time in all our years in the bosom of Lavrenty Pavlovich, we slept with fringes.

The next day, the entire orphanage, from young to old, washed at the bath house and was clothed in clean underwear. On the morning of the 23rd, a covered car drove into the yard, accompanied by guards. Soldiers began carrying bales tied up with twine into Dzerzhinsky hall. We realized that today, something was going to happen.

Over breakfast, Screwface solemnly announced that our old clothes were going to be replaced with a new uniform. We were divided into two groups: mites and pipsqueaks would get the uniform today, right after breakfast, while the lads and dudes would get it tomorrow. The entire orphanage became excited – we were eager to see this present from the people's commissar Beria. But before dinner, which was delayed by one and a half hours, the mites who were driven into Felix's hall were not allowed out. We only saw their uniform at dinner time. We liked the uniform. The grey shirt with turnover collar, the black pants, which were not yet trousers but no longer baggy pants, with a double band and two pockets, a lined jacket made of black "devil's leather", or kersey, with an inner pocket like sharp guys had.

We were dressed only before bedtime. Compared with the former variegated clothes, the new clothes really did look like a uniform. With our identical fringes, wearing it we looked like the molded articles of a mighty state machine. Only the buttons on the coats spoiled the impression. They were all different.

BERIA'S GIFT

The next day, Auntie Mashka told us in secret that tomorrow the pupils would be photographed, and that in the hall under the portrait of Dzerzhinsky, Themis was setting up all sorts of stands, and screwing powerful lamps into the light-holders. On the morning of April the 24th, the head supervisor, speaking across the entire scoffery, ordered for everyone to appear in fifteen minutes in the assembly hall in full uniform. In the hall, under the portrait of the goat-bearded one, we saw the throne-chair of our boss on a two-tiered platform hammered together by the workman. Lower down, around it, chairs were ranged. To the left, to the right and behind the throne, a four-tiered structure of benches was placed. In the center, opposite the boss's place, towered a solid box on three legs, covered with a black cloth. Not everyone knew that it was a camera.

Screwface arranged the orphans on the benches. On the highest bench, the dudes stood, and on the lowest bench the mites sat. During the photography, everyone was supposed to raise their heads and look at the top of the box, the upper rows were to stand "at attention", and the sitting mites were to put their hands on their knees. Screwface rehearsed with us for over an hour to achieve his favorite uniformity, replacing one boy with another because of a difference in height, or because their faces didn't suit each other. He paraded before us like his Toad did before her canvases, creating the picture he wanted with us, a picture of enormous size with figures of natural height. By the arrival of Toad and her entourage, we were barely staying on our feet.

Behind the cavalcade, there was a small, funny ginger bald man, who resembled at the same time Vladimir Ilich Lenin and a clown from a book about the circus. When he appeared, all the orphans lined up laughed involuntarily. The boss evidently thought that they were laughing about her, and stopping, she hissed angrily at Screwface:

"What's this outrage then?"

The supervisor went red and shouted at us:

"Silence! Stop it! Attention!" And for some reason he started hitting himself on his trousers.

We quieted down, but we could not turn our eyes away from the ginger bald-headed man. When the man ran up to the box on legs, we realized that he was the photographer. Jumping onto a low stool, he stuck his head into the black cloth, fussed about under it for a while, then grabbed the box, rested it on his shoulder and dragged it away, placing it right in the doorway. Meanwhile, Toad and her servants arranged themselves on the enormous platform under the portrait of the founder of the Cheka, the original state secret-police agency. The bald photographer once more climbed up on the stool, crawled under the cloth, removed the round cap from the wide brass pipe with glass and lisped:

"Wight, get weady…"

Once more, we couldn't stop ourselves – we burst out laughing. Screwface went wild again, threw down his chair next to Toad and running to the camera, shouted:

"What are you laughing about, little runts?! The committee has given you a present. Now, look at my fist!"

And holding it above the box, he growled:

"At the signal 'pli!' everyone freeze, got it? Photographer, get ready! One, two, pli!"

We froze. The bald man pressed the shutter.

"We'll repeat it again twice. One, two, pli!"

At the final "Wight!" we didn't laugh.

For two more days, the funny photographer photographed each of us individually. He was helped by curly-haired boys of fifteen or sixteen. Judging by the color of their hair, they were his sons. The red-haired family made excellent personal photos.

The collective photograph was taken into the assembly hall before the celebration. It looked lavish, and everyone rushed to see it. We had difficulty finding ourselves – we were all groomed to look identical. The most recognizable people in the large photograph were the bosses, especially the elevated Toad. Compared to her, the orphans looked like Lilliputians from the same brood.

On the 9th of May, in the yard, during the ceremonial formation in honor of Victory Day, as a present from Lavrenty Pavlovich we were each given one personal photograph in a triangular army envelope. These photos were the first possession that any of us owned. I was able to preserve mine and hold on to it through years of tribulations.

When in August I fled from the orphanage to my native Petersburg, the photograph was sewn into the lapel of my jacket, and in the pockets of my pants there were two coils of copper wire. One for a profile of Stalin, the other for a profile of Lenin. My copper leaders helped me survive, but that's another story.

Part 2
WIRE LEADERS

Without a house, without a nest,
I'm a homeless wanderer.
O, Fate, my fate,
You're black like a cat...
    (Orphan song)

THE BRONZE HORSEMAN

Mashka Cow Leg had a goat that always grazed in the field behind the kitchen, and besides grass, leaves and nettles, other things occasionally came its way as well. We also often hung around there, and competed with the slingshot. Additionally, we had a wonderful form of entertainment called "riding the goat". Don't think that it's easy – it's not easy at all, it's very difficult. I, for example, never once managed it. But I don't count – I was too skinny and light. The others – the normal boys – also tried it, but few of them succeeded. The goat bucked, and so powerfully and suddenly that many boys flew into the air and fell into the grass, and the ones who were especially clumsy received marks from her horns. But still, this was a very enticing game for us. Pete senior was the best at riding the goat (we had another two Petes – second and third).

Envious boys said that he had a heavy bottom. But I noticed that he had a certain dexterity: as he ran up, he would grab the goat by the horns and suddenly jump up on it. The goat's back legs even bent under him. In a word, Pete was known as the best rider, and we were proud of him and felt profound respect for him. He was also aware of his own importance and was declared to be a "senior" by all the dudes. Besides, he was already ten years old.

Once, when we were all hanging around by the kitchen, and as usual playing "goat", our boss, Toad, suddenly came out the kitchen door into our yard. And at that moment, Pete was astride the goat in a victorious pose. The NKVD artist swiftly grabbed him by the ear, and led him to her office/ workshop, repeating in her quacking little voice: "I'll show you such a goat, bronze horseman, that you'll find out what's what." At that time, we didn't know anything about the bronze horseman, and none of us had ever seen it, not even in a dream. But this title that Toad gave was terribly appropriate for Peter senior. Since then he was called the Bronze Horseman.

It was with him, the boy with a title, that I ran away from the orphanage to my homeland – to Petersburg, that is. Leningrad. Or rather, he ran away with me, because I was a shadow. My nickname was Shadow. The boys called me this because I was skinny and transparent. He was a Horseman, and a Bronze one at that, while I was just a shadow, but together we fled to my Leningrad from Chernoluchi, on the Irtysh, near the city of Omsk.

He had two reasons for running away. The first, of course, was Toad, whom he hated for the humiliation and pain she had caused him. And the second, main reason, was that he did not eat enough at the orphanage, as he thought himself, although he ate a lot more than we did. But he thought that in another place, especially in Leningrad, he would be fed much better, as they had starved in the war, but now, rumor had it, everyone ate well there. And since we had also starved, they would be sure to feed us well.

Pete was talented at finding things, and had an incredible sense of smell for food. It was inexplicable how he sensed where it was necessary to go to be witness to the ingestion of edibles, and to partake in it. He successfully presented me as a "victim of famine". I think that he took me with him because of my dystrophy, to profit from it – seeing this "shadow", a scarfer could not help sharing with us. And as soon as we got our share, it disappeared with incredible swiftness in Pete's belly. I was usually the observer, and if I got a portion of the food, it was exactly the amount needed to continue living.

It didn't take him any effort to convince me to run away. Especially as Toad persecuted me because of the wire portraits. The war had come to an end, and I thought that my mother Bronya would already be there, in Leningrad, and I could return to her. And I would speak Polish again. Besides, Pete was the Horseman, and I was his Shadow. We escaped on a barge that delivered groceries to various places along the Irtysh. The NKVD orphanage also received its share from the barge with our help. We carried the groceries from the jetty to the kitchen, and knew the arrangement of the barge in the inside very well.

The trip on the barge was uninteresting. We hid in the hold, among empty grocery boxes, and slept with the rats. The rats were warm and well-fed – not dangerous. My Horseman, who quickly ate the food he had taken with him, regretted several times that he had fled from the ration, but it was too late.

After various ordeals – hunger, cold – we reached the Remote Place (OMSK). Pete's talent led us to the Omsk train station. He felt inside that there would be food there, that we would be fed there, and that we would travel along the railroad further to the west, to my Petersburg. We did not come to the train station itself, but to the sorting part, and found ourselves among the wagons with soldiers, who as it turned out were travelling from the German front to the Japanese front. The Omsk wagons were being hitched to theirs. And between the wagons, we unexpectedly ran into a strangely merry "drinking" train that did not resemble the others. From behind the train's barred windows, we could see shaved soldiers heads looking greedily at everything taking place outside. Only one of the wagons was open, and there was great merriment going on inside. "Probably the bosses' wagon," we thought.

From this freight car, we were noticed, or rather I was noticed first.

"Hey, look what a consumptive stray just blew in," I heard someone say.

Another tipsy guy asked:

"Kid, hey kid, who made you so thin?"

Pete was immediately begging behind me, saying that we were starving, "didn't the guys have anything for us to eat?"

"Well, look what a rosy-cheeked smarty just showed up! Hey, little goat, what are you hiding behind this scrap for?" the eldest of them croaked. "You don't look as if you were starving. You squeezed everything out of your little friend here, but you're doing quite all right for yourself, chubby. A real goat! All right them, come here, get in with us! We'll feed you all right. And bring your 'consumption' with you!"

All of them, dressed in soldiers' uniforms, were somehow different from the other ordinary soldiers. And they behaved in the freight car as if they owned the place, as if they were the ones in charge in this "merry" train and were acting like lords, that is, drinking, playing cards and ignoring the guards.

While we were being fed, I noticed that the men were carnivorously looking Peter over, even pinching him, slapping him on the bottom, saying: "That's an appetizing little rump you've grown there, eh!" I started to feel uneasy. Sensing that something was wrong, I nudged my friend several times, but he was busy eating, and uninterested in anything but food. I saw tattoos on their arms, and it also seemed to me that the card game was connected with us, that is with him, Pete – my suspicious cough scared them off. I nudged Pete in the side again and suggested we go outside to answer the call of nature. He continued eating greedily. Despairing of directing his attention to the dangerous oddities, coughing, I asked to go outside for "number one" (nearby, under the wagon) – and ran away. I ran in real fear from this feeding, ran from the word "goat", the terrifying criminal meaning of which I learned soon after this incident. I ran from this evil, I ran to Leningrad, not knowing that it had its own bronze horseman there.

Much later, when I was an adult, I heard from a guy in the military that Marshal Malinovsky, who had commanded the Baikal front in the Japanese campaign, himself a former criminal, on the first night of the war with the samurais, without warning the superiors, without artillery preparation, which the Japanese were waiting for, threw at them the hardened criminals who had been selected in our prisons and camps. With knives, without a single shot, they butchered the Japanese who were sleeping in the first line of trenches, part of the Kwantung Army. They say that almost all the prisoners were killed by our own bullets, but they made their contribution and determined the success of the attack by the Soviet troops. Perhaps this did not happen, but when I heard the story from the soldier who had apparently seen it for himself, I remembered the terrifying "merry" echelon on the Omsk rails and Pete the horseman, turned into a "goat".

I only saw the real Bronze Horseman seven years later.

PICTURES OF MEMORY

From Omsk to the west, to the Urals, there were two branches: one in the direction of Sverdlovsk, the northern branch, and the other to Chelyabinsk, the southern branch. I did not make a choice, I didn't even know which one was better for me, and I ended up on the Chelyabinsk branch. Having got onto a platform with empty containers, out of sheer fright I blew through several sections, to the station Isilkul, where the train was put on a reserve track and I had to climb out of my hiding place. My final destination was not Chelyabinsk, but remote Petersburg, and I was travelling there in a new state uniform, sewn for Victory Day by prison seamstresses. In the pockets of my pants there was a stolen spoon, a small sharpening slate, a slingshot, which I had made myself at the orphanage night amnesties, and two spools of cooper wire, carefully measured for two profiles – Comrade Stalin and Comrade Lenin.

The art of bending the profiles of our leaders, which I learnt at the orphanage, saved me from starvation throughout my six-year journey through stations, towns and villages, through the orphanages and colonies from Siberia to Leningrad. At train stations, restaurants, canteens, buffets, bazaars and markets, the frontline people who had won the Great Patriotic War could not refuse food to a hungry boy, especially not for the profiles of their beloved leaders that he fashioned before their eyes out of copper wire, especially of the generalissimo.

In these tempestuous travelling months of 1945, as I moved towards the Urals, I became increasingly familiar with the completely special world of the railroad. An enormous military armada was moving from the Urals to the Japanese front. Endless echelons of freight cars with soldiers and platforms with tanks, artillery and other equipment, under canvas and uncovered, travelled across the country. In the opposite direction, from the Far East to the Urals and beyond, entire trains of empty platforms, cisterns and freight cars travelled, to be occupied once more with endless weapons, ammunition and fuel; and with soldiers again. A new Japanese war was being prepared. To Siberia, from the Great Patriotic War, soldiers and officers returned, late because of their treatment in hospital, with stumps of arms and legs wrapped in bandages, with burns, with mutilated faces cracked with injuries – living documents of the war. At every station and substation, they were met by bawling women, who collected their own dear fighters, and took them home.

The restaurants of large stations had put out tables and chairs on the platforms, and just before the arrival of the passenger trains, the waitresses poured hot beetroot borshch, the dream of the stomach, from a pot into white soup bowls. The bar girl bustled around among the beer mugs, filling them up, letting the foam settle and once more pouring out the golden drink.

The arriving train threw out hungry humanity in soldiers' shirts and jackets. It immediately filled up the platform restaurant, and the tribal eating of the native dish began, Siberian borshch. Only requests and orders could be heard: "Girls, another beer, dears, some more borshch, my beauties, two of the largest beers, and salt". Frontline invalids of all types threw a pinch of salt in their beer mugs before they drank. An explosion took place in the mug –the foam rose suddenly, and the drinker vanished into it, greedily swallowing the golden sweetness of life. Some of them, particularly sophisticated, sprinkled the edge of the mug with salt, and turning it, drank the beer through this salt. It seemed to me that these people crippled by the war lacked salt to restore the body parts they had lost.

The waitresses were extremely popular among the frontline men who were starving for female affection. Each one wanted at least to touch the fancied-up female wonder and call the woman by an affectionate, diminutive name.

From almost every train that came from the west, one of the soldiers carried out to the platform an accordion, usually a trophy accordion, and treated the feasting soldiers to "Katyusha", "Zemlyanka" or "Three Tank Crew Soldiers". And from above, from the wall of the train station, from an enormous portrait with his post-war smile at the victorious people, gazed the great leader, the generalissimo in a white marshal's uniform in full regalia.

On the restaurant walls and in the waiting halls hung endless variations of Shishkin's "Bears", Kuindzhi's "Birch Groves" and Perov's "Hunters at Rest", reproduced with an incomplete set of paints by unknown artisans.

The train stations, platforms, squares by the stations and the space around them in the towns and villages along the entire route of the echelons were filled with people from all ethnic groups possible in Russia, all languages, ages, types and ranks. They sat on suitcases, chests, boxes, slept on sacks and God only knows on what else and how. All of this humanity made a terrible racket, snored, chewed, rustled, argued among themselves, laughed and roared – in a word, they lived and hurried as they waited for their trains. At this "bazaar", you could hear anything at all. One woman complained to another:

"I've been completely deprived of a head of the household, first my husband, then the eldest, the medium-aged, and in '44 the youngest son was called to the front. I don't remember, I don't remember at all, I remember one funeral after another... There hasn't been a final one, and so I go to meet the trains. God grant that I'll be able to greet at least oneof my own."

In a crowd of very drunk guys, some shaggy old man, talking to an enormous lanky fellow, said:

"If a Ukrainian isn't a khokhol, a Russian isn't a Moskal, a Pole isn't a Polack, then I'm a Jew, but not a Yid. You hear what I, Yevsey, am telling you, you understand me?"

"Shut up, Yesya. You've drunk too much and you're blathering, don't talk crap, don't rend the air," the enormous fingerless robber said in a fatherly way to the old man.

On the train station bench, a tender woman rustled around her crippled husband, speaking to a pock-marked, envious single woman:

"Let the legs go, the main thing is that the gag works, for a woman it's worse without a gag, what's smooth, what needs satin-stitching – it's all the same. He doesn't talk much, but he's good with his hands, he does everything well. What's more, a legless man isn't going to run away, and I'll do the talking. I spent three days rushing to get to him, hurrying. Oh, my God, my God, a Communist, a Party member, but without legs. The bosses of the collective farm promised to send a car for you. My breath, my lover-boy. What are you cocking your ears for? I'm complaining to him, you have nothing to do with it."

"Instead of lovey-doveying, you should feed him. The guy's looking with his mouth, he doesn't hear anything."

"Don't be afraid, I'll feed him, I've brought a whole basket, and we have a wheelchair. We have a grown daughter, she also baked pies. He's good with his hands, he can do everything, and we'll give him wheels instead of legs. Right, Vasechka? Oh, my precious one!"

"Klava, Klava, pour me a cup, my soul wants it, you hear, my soul wants it! Klava…"

To this crowd of people, every day womenfolk of various ages were added, coming to the trains. Just to look, sympathize, envy… who, what, why, what for… Lacking any cinema, they watched the cinema of life. Most of them were not there for any reason, just to look at the soldiers going by, and participate in the joys as the front-line soldier returned to his homeland. And just in case, in case some one of the passers-by would endow them with his desires, his tales.

MOTHER OF GOD…

From various pictures, the memory of my eyes has kept one that is quite unexpected. Glimpsing the head of her man in the window, a young, strong Siberian woman jumped onto the sideboard of the still moving train, and shoving aside a crowd of soldiers in the vestibule, she rushed inside. Some time after the train stopped, she appeared in the doorway of the wagon, beautiful, black-eyed, holding in her arms, like a child, a legless, one-armed cripple in a striped shirt. He, embracing the woman with his one arm, looked at her with blue, guilty eyes, and intoned in a bass voice:

"Forgive me, Nyusha, I couldn't stay safe, I couldn't stay safe…"

"Mother of God, Mother of God, Jesus Christ!" shrieked a perpetually drunk old woman, crossing herself as she looked at them and falling to her knees before the wagon.

The crowd was stunned.

Two soldiers carefully took the "Mother of God" with her burden off the sideboard of the wagon, and put her on the platform. The black-eyed woman, striding into the parted crowd, carried her mutilated little christ through the people, bawling and laughing with joy at the same time. Some one sighed:

"War…"

THE FIRST RATION

Having wound up in Isilkul and starving after my journey, I made my way along the railway lines filled with military wagons, toward the train station, in the hope of finding food. The soldiers noticed me from the open wagons, and called to me:

"Hey boy, what are you wandering around here for?"

"I'm going to the station, I want to earn some food."

"How are you going to earn it, lad?"

"By art."

"What art?"

"I bend profiles of leaders."

"What? How do you do that? Show us!"

"If you feed me, I'll show you."

"We'll feed you, we'll feed you, don't worry."

I stopped, took the Stalin twist of wire out of the right pocket of my pants, and began to twist the leader out of it before their eyes. While I worked, the soldiers silently watched my hands. And when I had finished and showed it to them, they admitted that it looked just like Stalin did on medals, and they rewarded me with a good ration – almost a whole loaf of bread and a lump of delicious lard.

"Where are you from?"

"From Leningrad, I'm going home with my mother, but she fell ill, and I had to become the breadwinner."

In the evening at a canteen not far from the station, I earned some more. After I'd stocked up on food, I snuck into the passenger train to Kurgan by night, and fell asleep on the upper baggage shelf of a general wooden wagon between baskets, suitcases and bundles. Thus my flight from Omsk to the west continued – I was only fleeing to the west.

ESCAPE FROM
THE BLACK RASPBERRY

I was wakened in the morning by noise. There was a search underway in the wagon. A police railroad patrol, along with the train conductors, was clearing out the train. I was miraculously able to climb along the third-tier shelves between the ceiling and the pipes that divided the coupe, into the part of the old wagon that had already been checked, and at the stop, climbing down into the corridor, I went out onto the platform along with the passengers. The station turned out to be quite a big one, and I decided to stay there. I spent my day in curious investigation. I went to the local market and stood there by a guy who was cutting silhouettes from life out of black paper, and doing it so well that I really envied him. If only I could learn such a trade! I spent the night at the train station in the waiting hall, finding a place between two families with children, and I slept with my head tucked into my jacket. My inoffensive face and the fringe that Lavernty Pavlovich had given me as a gift for Victory Day gave me a domestic look, and I didn't arouse any particular suspicion among the people at the train station. If anyone asked me why I was by myself at the station, I lied: "The doctors took Mama away for treatment, I don't have anywhere to go, we're not from here, we're going back to Petersburg." Many people took pity on me and fed me as if I was part of their family.

The next morning, when I tried to get into the second wagon of a passenger train that was going in the direction of the Urals, out of inexperience I found myself in the clutches of the black-raspberry uniformed railway police. At the police station I lied once more that on the way from Novosibirsk, my Petersburg grandmother had died, and that I was trying to return home without her. On the second day, a young cop took me to the canteen (at the police station the detainees were fed once a day). The canteen, where I had earned food the day before with my profiles, was in a spacious wooden building with a hall, entrance rooms and a porch. After we ate, I asked to go to the toilet. The policeman, relaxed by food, let me go, and went onto the porch to smoke a cigarette, from where the wooden booth could be seen. The back of the outhouse adjoined the neighboring fence. When I opened the door and saw a little window cut out in the board in the back wall above the toilet, I realized that I would be able to squeeze through it, and that I had better get going. I really didn't want to see Toad and Screwface again. Through the neighboring overgrown lot, crouching down, I went out onto a side street, and by intuition or somehow – I can't explain it myself – I moved not toward the village, but to the rails, to the goods trains, where I had arrived two days ago. I crawled under the tarpaulin that covered a self-propelled gun and, out of fear, I slept under it for the rest of the day. This maneuver saved me: they obviously looked for me in the village, and not among the soldiers, by the technical equipment. Once more, I slipped through their fingers, justifying my orphanage nicknames – the Shadow and the Invisible Man.

After this incident, I figured out that at large stations, with railway police, it was dangerous to get into the first wagons without a ticket, or to emerge from them. A group of cops is usually hanging about at the head of the train. It's better to walk down the train and exit onto the platform from the end of it. But it's not advisable to get into the last wagon either, because the conductor keeps a man there who is specially instructed to look out for thieves. Which I soon experienced for myself.

At night I was able to get into a goods train that was slowly moving in my direction, to the west. On it I reached the next hub station.

AN INHERITANCE FROM A THIEF

My empty goods train was once more driven into a dead-end, and I set off towards the train station square, where I witnessed the catching of a train thief. Or rather, two thieves, but I only saw one of them being caught with my own eyes. Five plain-clothes policemen chased two guys from the platform to the station square and the streets that fanned out from it. The thieves separated when they reached the streets. Three cops chased the thief to my right, and two chased the other, along the neighboring street. The trinity caught up with the guy. From out of the bushes where I was hiding, I could see that he fell to the ground in a special way, thief-like, having fallen to the ground and turned on his head, he kicked one of the pursuers over, but the other two came crashing down on him and didn't let him get up. While he was tumbling over, I noticed that something was thrown from him and fell into the grass. In the struggle, the cops didn't notice this. When the thief had been taken to the station, I fossicked in the grass and found two train passkeys tied up with twine. Much later, I discovered that if keys or lock picks had been found on the thief, then his sentence would have been doubled. The second thief probably escaped from his pursuers – he jumped over the tall fence of a private house very nimbly. Thus, I inherited two wagon passkeys, and they helped me to survive. They had to be used carefully, without letting anyone see them; in time I sewed a bag for them with ties on it, and kept it tied to my leg.

MY FRIEND MITYAI

On the stretch from Kara-Gug to the large hub station of Asanovo in the Omsk-Chelyabinsk passenger train, made up of old, antediluvian wagons filled to the gunnels with a motley bunch of people moving from one place to another, I met my sidekick in my further travels to the Ural, and the first friend in my life, whom I loved with my orphan's heart as if he were my brother. I met him in a quite unexpected place, or rather we were introduced – in the train vestibule. I don't know what got into me, but some devil made me take my profiles to the last wagon, at that time I already knew that it was dangerous. The ferocious conductor grabbed me there and dragged me by my collar into the back vestibule of his wagon, in the train holding cell. Pushing me into the dark dungeon on wheels, with metal-covered doors, he growled:

"Here's a friend for you, say hello. At the next station I'll hand you two beggars over to the police, you wait."

As soon as the conductor locked the door, I told the boy that I had passkeys to the train doors, and that we would be able to clear out. When the train approached the station, we'd open the door, climb out onto the steps, and as soon as it slowed down, we'd jump – and off we'd run.

"I won't be able to jump…"

"What's the problem, it's easy and not scary at all, this is the last wagon, as soon as it reaches the platform, then you can jump."

"I'm blind… I'm blind Mitka, I can't jump."

After he said that, having got used to the darkness, in the chink of light I could make out that the boy's face was mutilated. In his left eye socket there was no eye, and from his right eye-socket, under a scar that came down from his forehead, something was hanging.

"Why didn't he pity you, the viper? Why did he lock you in here?"

"For singing, I asked for food and sang. I went through all the wagons, no one bothered me, even the conductor ladies gave me bread, but this one grabbed me by the collar and threw me in here."

"The blood-sucker! But don't be scared, we'll pull one over on him. As soon as the train slows down, I'll open the outside door, I'll go down to the lower step and help you, I'll take you by the hand. We'll run away from the wagon and hide behind the far-off trains. I'm already experienced. The main thing is, he doesn't get here first. Let's stick something in the lock."

"What's your name?" the blind boy asked.

"Stepanych, after my father. I'll feel around in the stoker, maybe there's something we can use there. If we even fill the lock hole with coal, then while he's trying to open it, we'll have time to escape. I'll also try to close the door from the outside, then the bastard will really be stuck. Mitka, are you a local?"

"No, I'm from the Novgorod area."

"That's excellent! We'll travel together. I'm from Leningrad – right next door. How did you end up in Siberia?"

"When we were evacuated, our train was destroyed by German planes. My mother and little brother were killed, and I was injured, as you can see. My aunt survived. She was the one who took me to Siberia. We lived near Novosibirsk. To start with everything was fine – she fed me. Then, toward the end of the war, she got involved with a policeman and started begrudging me food. She called me a sponger. And so I left. I started singing songs at markets, and staying in people's entryways. Now the war's over, I've decided to go home. My grandpa and grandma stayed behind, maybe they're still alive. In Novosibirsk, a poor old man taught me train songs. He made himself out as my guide, took all the money for himself and drank it. I ran away from him. My right eye can see a little, I thought, I won't stumble. People started giving me more for my work. How do you feed yourself?

"I make art. I make profiles of leaders out of wire in front of people's eyes. The guys from the front like it – they feed me, sometimes they even give me money."

"That's amazing! How do you do it?"

I took out the twist of wire for the generalissimo, and after a while I gave him the profile. He started feeling it, saying: "Well done, that's great!" – and suddenly said to me:

"Stepanych, what if we work together? You make your leaders out of wire, and I'll sing about them? Let's try it. I know three songs about Stalin. If we're together it will be easier and safer, beggars keep bothering me, last week I was almost maimed. They want me to work for them."

"Don't worry, Mityai, I've got a slingshot for them, we can maim them ourselves."

At the next stop we successfully escaped from the vestibule prison. We circled behind our wagon, ducked under a stationary military train, then under another, and ended up on the free side of the station, where there was nothing apart from barns. Running my eyes over the tracks, I saw empty wagons in the far corner, which had saved me several times already. Mityai and I ran over to them and took cover in one of them. We would have to wait until nightfall, and not stick our heads out. The conductor had probably raised the alarm. He would have given our description to the station officials. Officers would start searching on all the tracks. Thank God dusk was falling, it would be harder to look for us at night, in the dark.

Several minutes later, we finally heard the banging of the shields on the buffers, and our miserable train moved away from the station.

Until it got completely dark, we decided to scoff from our common stores. And our brotherly supper was glorious. His bread with my lard from the soldiers, and his boiled potatoes in a cabbage leaf adorned what was left of our perilous day. From satiety and nervous fatigue we soon relaxed and fell asleep on some remains of straw.

We woke up from a crash: our wagons were being dragged somewhere. I looked out – we were being connected to another empty line of heated freight cars and platforms. In forty minutes, this entire mass on wheels fortunately moved west. I already knew by that time that empty trains did not travel more than two or three stretches. They were moved at times when there were no military trains, which were being driven east. At the next stop we would have to wait somewhere, so that we were forgotten on that stretch of the railway.

The middle of August was approaching. It was warm. We travelled through a forest steppe zone. More and more often, we encountered Kazakh nomad camps. The cicadas and fantastic aromas of the night steppe made our heads spin from their unfamiliarity.

MONSTERS

On the way, Mityai told me a horrifying story about a band of beggars who got their hands on him in Omsk and earned good money from him, and drank this money, beating him up for nothing. It didn't seem enough to them that Mityai was blind and that his face was mutilated by shell fragments. So that people would feel even more pity for him, they decided to cut off his right hand. He was lucky that he accidentally overheard them conspiring. Meanwhile, past the collective farm hay-drying house, where the monstrous brothers were sleeping, a cart was travelling along the road to the station – a man was taking his wife and daughter to the morning train. By the sound, Mityai realized that someone was going by. In the darkness, he was able to slip away from the bandit beggars and run up to the cart. Grabbing the shaft of the cart, he shouted:

"Uncle, uncle, take me with you, or they'll cut off my hand! I'm blind Mitka, save me, save me!"

At first the driver didn't have a clue what was going on. Then, when he saw two tramps pulling away the boy holding on to the shaft, he realized that things were serious. He took a rifle out of the straw where he had hidden it away in case of any emergencies, and shot into the air to scare them off. The guys backed away from Mitka, but started shouting that he was their nephew, and demanded that he be handed over.

"Don't give me to them, uncle, I'm not their nephew, please don't! They'll cut off my hand! They pretend to be beggars, they drink vodka and beat me. It's not enough for them that I'm blind and crippled, they want more..."

"I'll shoot those utter sons of bitches, that outhouse carrion, like fascist swine! I've got a wooden leg myself. Look, boy, since '42 I've walked with a piece of wood instead of a leg."

The man shot the rifle into the darkness a second time. The guys threw themselves down in the road and crawled into the ditch.

That beggar scum could have done anything to Mitka: gouged out his other eye, torn off a piece of his nose, or his lips, cut off his hand or foot, or his tongue so that he couldn't talk but only grunt. Then, putting this miserable monster in a box, they would have dragged him from town to town, squeezing the last pennies out of people's pity and kindness.

My guardian angels saved me from that sort of carrion. But in my travels I saw this perverted human filth that hunts children like animals, robs them, rapes them, and then disfigures them with a ferocity that the devil wouldn't dream of. This brotherhood is terribly cowardly. At one station on the way to Chelyabinsk, two beggar women, pretending to be nuns, cast their greedy eyes on Mitka and tried to drag him away from me:

"We'll be your guides, we'll feed you and look after you, we'll make a man of you and make your life easier. And you skinny boy, get out of here, don't get in our way, or we'll waste you!" And they showed me a shank.

I shouted, furious:

"Don't touch him, you old bitches, or I'll blow you up with a grenade – you'll go flying in pieces!" And grabbing a dark brown bottle of water out of my bag, I went after them. They ran off.

Another time, there was a brazen, revolting old man who was after Mitka, and I shot him in the jaw with a wire bullet from my catapult. After that he immediately vanished whenever he saw us.

BATS

After three stretches of track, our rumbling train of empty freight cars stopped on a reserve track in some forest steppe station. We woke up from the silence. It was morning. All the tracks turned out to be filled up with trains like ours. It was essential for Mitka and me to get out of the wagon without being noticed, without being seen by the railway people, and disappear for three or four days. We shifted the heavy door together, jumped on to the ground, and crawled under our wagon to the other side. We passed several more trains in the same way. Once we found ourselves past the tracks of our station,

I saw the bend of a river half a kilometer from the road, and beyond it a grove or forest. We were lucky again – we could wash ourselves, even swim, and most importantly wait for a while, so that later, once we had earned some food, we could move west. As I reached the river, I saw some sort of abandoned structure beyond the bend, built almost above the water, and the remains of old wooden piles in the water, covering the entire river. I had never seen such a construction before. Mitka suggested from my description that it was an old mill. We decided to swim in the mill pond first of all, then investigate the mill as a possible place to spend the night. At noon, the local boys came to swim. They weren't surprised to see us. They only asked:

"Did you come from the trains?"

"Yes, we stopped."

"That's typical. Sometimes the trains can stand there for weeks."

From them, we found out that once there used to be a village in this area, but it had moved to the station long ago, beyond the train terminal. Only the mill remained. They said of the forest that it was very large, and continued to the north along the river, and that at one time there were even wolves living in it.

We slept in the attic of the mill. I woke up early in the morning from fright. Into the empty window space, one after another, frightening black winged shadows flew, and disappeared in the darkness of the high attic roof. At first I thought that I was still asleep and dreaming a strange, fantastic dream. I tried to shake it off, but I could not. How do you like that: you can't wake up, and they keep flying in. I threw myself on the sleeping Mitka and started shaking him, saying:

"Look, look, what's that?", forgetting that he could not see.

"What are you bothering me for, you know I can't see anything but a bit of light," Mityai complained, waking up. "My grandma in the country said something about flying spirits, but I don't know who these flying beasts of yours are."

It wasn't until the daytime that we heard from a local boy that they were bats, and that they were not dangerous to people, but lived here since the old times, in the attic of the mill. At night they hunted for insects, but slept during the day, clinging to the rafters of the roof with their wing-claws.

Our food supplies lasted for three days. For three days we slept, swam, lay in the sun and prepared for our performances together. It was important for me to get the trick of bending the leader's profile toward the end of his songs, not earlier and not later. Finally it all started to come together.

ALLOWED – NOT ALLOWED

On the fourth day, we had to go to the station to earn some bread. The station turned out to be quite large, with a restaurant at the terminal and tables on the platform. There was a rather large square behind the train station, filled with cars, carts, and people coming to meet or see off their soldiers.

We held our first joint performance on this station square, and were successful. For the first time, people asked me in addition to bend a profile of Lenin, and for Mitka to sing "Katyusha" – and were very happy. They fed us and gathered a whole bundle of food for us. After two days of working at the station, we turned into local celebrities. The boys who swam in the river boasted to everyone that they knew us.

The next day we tried to perform on the station platform, and almost ended up in the clutches of the railway police. The canteen lady at the platform restaurant knew about us from the boys who hung around us, and allowed us to work among the tables. In the middle of the day, a passenger train arrived at the station from the west, and released a crowd of hungry soldiers onto the platform. The drinking of beer and eating of borshch commenced.

I took the Stalin twist of wire out of my jacket, straightened it out and addressed the men who were already enjoying the taste of beer:

"Dear saviors of the nation, comrade soldiers and officers, allow us to sing about the leader comrade Stalin and show him in profile for a small bite to eat."

Mitka sang in his high voice, raising to the sky his head, disfigured by bomb fragments:

> Stalin is our military glory,
> Stalin is our pride and gives us wings...

As soon as I started bending the generalissimo's nose, suddenly the black uniform of a railway police toadstool appeared on the platform. Pulling his cap with the raspberry top down over his forehead, he walked straight towards us. Mitka sang:

With songs, in battle and in triumph
Our people follow Stalin…

I had reached the leader's chin. The cop stopped between the tables opposite us, puffed up his cheeks in a crimson bubble and yelled:

"Stop it! It's not allowed, I tell you!"

The army at the tables around him rose to its feet, and a head lieutenant said in a voice trembling from contusion:

"What's that?... It's not allowed to sing about the leader?... And according to… article… 58… do you know what's allowed?!"

And he looked at the toadstool cop with his single ferocious eye. Another soldier, higher in rank, ordered the backline rat to clear off, which he immediately did.

Mitya and I performed everything before the army, but realized that as soon as the train started moving we would be put in the hoosegow, and so before the train left, we jumped off the platform and ran across the rails to the other side of the station, so the cop didn't see us.

The next morning, two of the local boys we already knew came to our place in the mill and told us that yesterday the police had been looking for us at the station, and had even asked if anyone knew where we had gone.

So that's how it was! That meant our fears were quite justified. We would once more have to lie low for a while.   It was probably even imperative that we disappear from the mill. We asked the boys to tell everyone that they saw us on the sideboard of a train leaving, but in the opposite direction.

We took our possessions and food from the mill, and went into the forest to wait there for three or four days, afterwards to return by night to the railroad, and hiding in an empty goods car, move on to Chelyabinsk.

FOREST WOLVES

Climbing along the river's edge on an overgrown path, after an hour and a half we reached a tiny clearing surrounded by tall trees and elevated above the river. Here we found a pit with the remains of a fire. The place was a convenient one, and we decided to stay there. We were also rather tired. Mitka fossicked around in the fire pit, and found several still-warm baked potatoes. This find did not alarm us, probably there were fishermen in these parts. A little further on, in the bushes, I saw a fine shanty. It was a whole camping ground. We didn't want to leave this place to go anywhere else, and we also didn't have any energy to do so. Evening had begun to fall. Come what may, we thought. We'd eat and spend the night there, and in the morning we would decide what to do next. There weren't any pirates living here, after all, and clearly not any cops around. Mitka started taking out food and putting in on the stump, and I broke up some dried branches and threw them into the pit, intending to light a fire with the last, precious matches.

As soon as I had kneeled and bent over to ignite the branches, out of the bushes from the side of the river two human shapes appeared in long hooded raincoats, in boots, and one of them had a stick in his hand. We initially froze in fright and stared at them. Who were they? Pharaoh bosses or robbers, spirits of the taiga? Finally, one of them, who was shorter, with slanted eyes and a flat face, said in an unfamiliar dialect:

"Fire doesn't like disorder. You need to arrange a fire well, then light it."

After these words we felt instinctively, like puppies, that the men might be a bit unusual but they wouldn't harm us, we had nothing to fear. Emboldened, I asked them:

"Are you guys from the security services?"

"Where did you get that idea?" the tall man asked angrily.

"They walk around the wagons in coats just like those, guarding."

The men exchanged glances.

"Maybe you feed yourselves with fish, or from the forest?" I continued to ask.

"The forest and the devil. You can think of us as woodsmen, enough already!" the tall man replied. "How did you lads end up here, then? What are you doing alone in this place?"

"We need to wait things out for a while, we're on the run. The black raspberries are hunting us at the station. And we escaped from lockup before that."

I told them about all our adventures: how we had escaped from the train vestibule, from the evil cop, and how we had been saved by the soldiers from the police, and that we were being hunted, there had been an announcement at the station that two vagabond boys had slipped through their fingers, and one of them was blind. We had hid at the mill, but the cops found out about that too, and so we ran away. We were going to sit out the danger, then get in a goods car and…

"Look how experienced they are, they've worked it all out."

The slant-eyed man made a quick trip with a kettle to get some water, and taking the branches out of the fire pit, instantaneously laid a new fire and just as quickly, by striking together some kind of stones, ignited a twist of rope, with which he started the flames.

"Hey, that's interesting! I've never seen that before," I said in amazement.

As he got the fire going, he kept repeating:

"Runaway, runaway lads, how about that. Don't worry, we won't give you to p'lice." And he began to stroke the head of the blind boy. "What happened to him, was he shot?"

I told them Mitka's story.

"How about that, there you go, eh! Bunch of animals!"

The slant-eyed man took a lump of tea out of his roomy bag, and wrapping it in a rag, broke it up between two stones.

"Chinese tea, a Kazakh woman brought it, you drink it and get happy! I'm a Khanty, do you know who they are? No? Forest people."

"You make a great fire."

"You want I teach you?"

"Teach me."

102

"Ok, drink tea and I'll teach you, teach you today and teach you tomorrow. We'll give the blind boy tea first."

He sprinkled the broken tea into a mug, poured boiling water over it, mixed it with a trimmed twig, and along with a piece of bread covered in lard, he handed it to my friend:

"Drink, Mityai, Chinese tea is good. What's wrong – is it bitter? Never you mind if the tea's bitter. Drink it, you'll get used to it, life is bitter, but tea tastes good."

After the tea he started teaching us how to build fires.

I'll try to use my own words to retell the lessons that I was given sixty-five years ago in a forest that bordered the steppe not far from North Kazakhstan.

The first thing you should know is that fire obeys the sun. A tree rises from the butt-end to the sun. Fire also burns from the butt-end more quickly. When you pick up a twig, a branch, a log, look where the butt-end is. Secondly: you must find a fuse, especially in bad weather. A good fuse for lighting a fire is birch bark. Another good fuse is dry fir twigs. They can always be found under the lowest branches of a thick fir tree. You can squeeze the twigs into balls – and everything's ready. In rainy weather, this is powder for a fire.

Fires are chosen depending on the need and the weather. The simplest and quickest is the Khanty fire, the thick log fire, in Siberia it is called a thief's fire, because it burns without smoke. Water in a pot boils in four minutes over this fire.

Before you place the log, you must create the foundation of the fire – out of thick branches, not necessarily dry ones. At the foundation, you place a log – from the butt-end by the direction of the sun, and then the fire will wrap around the kettle. The lower part of the fire is made of thick branches, and the upper parts of thinner branches. Place the fuse inside. When the fuse has been lit, place small branches at angles to each other on top, without hurrying, until the fire catches.

Forest people can arrange a fire like this to heat a hut or tent, which after it gets going will burn of its own accord for five to six hours without having to look after it, and wet wood is even more preferable here. A cone-shaped pit is dug under this fire, and the logs are placed with the butt-end down, in a circle. The wettest and largest are on the outside of the pit, and towards the middle are drier bunches of wood. In the center there is a nest of dry branches, the fuse is placed here and lit. This fire burns slowly, it dries itself out, and the logs that burn from the bottom creep along the cone towards the fire. If such a fire is laid out at an angle towards the wind, it will heat a tent or hut all night and drive away the mosquitoes.

The Khanty showed us how to properly choose places for encampments in the forest, so that the earth wouldn't shift, and would remain dry, and how to orient a shanty according to the sun – so that the sun is at your head in the morning, and at your feet in the evening.

From him, we discovered that we needed to look for ants' nests – ants choose the safest places for living organisms, dry and stable. You can put a shanty next to an ants' nest, the main thing is not to destroy the ants' pathways of life. And then snakes will never crawl into the shanty or the tent, and neither will ticks. These vermin are afraid of going near ants.

From the behavior of birds, ants, bees and other living things, forest people can understand what the weather will be like, discover the proximity of dwellings, the approach of people, the appearance of danger and many other things.

Under the Khanty's guidance, according to all the rules of forest lore, I assembled and wove together a waterproof shanty, from a distance resembling a "yaranga", or tent made of reindeer hides.

When the evenings were cool, the men put on vests of goat fur over their shirts. I had never seen clothing like this before. They were rectangular pieces of goat hide with a hole for the head and laces sewn on the sides. When they crawled into the shanty to sleep, they took the vests off and put them under themselves, with the fur facing up. The Khanty, noticing my interest in their clothing, said that no snakes or insects would crawl onto goat's fur, and that warmth from below was more beneficial than warmth from above.

In the mornings, the men went off somewhere with their bags. They returned in the evening. Who they actually were and how they fed themselves was a mystery. Knowledgeable people whom I later told about this meeting in the forest suggested that they were hashish dealers. They supplied drugs to the north – to the prison colonies – from the steppe in the south. In short, they were involved in a very dangerous business, for which the punishment was execution in those times.

The Khanty took a tinderbox out of his bag, a tinder and flint, and taught me how to use them. He took some caulked moss out of a leather bag, and before my eyes he nimbly twisted together an extra fire-starting bundle, telling me to repeat all the actions after him, and then gave the tinderbox to us.

In secrecy from Mityai, he explained to me that my friend had problems with his lungs, and that he needed to be fed well, or even better we should get to a town as soon as we could and take Mityai to a lung doctor for treatment.

The man in charge told us to break camp the day after they left and disappear from the clearing, because real guards might come along. He showed me a path above our clearing, along which we could walk unseen through the forest, to the reserve railway tracks. He forbid us to return along the river. About them, should we get caught by the police, we weren't to say a word – we hadn't seen them, we didn't know them, we hadn't heard them. He ordered us to dismantle our shanty after they had left, and scatter the branches in different directions. There were fishermen camping here, not forest wolves.

The meeting with the forest people was a gift of fate, a school of survival in the open, in the forest, among nature. In subsequent orphan wandering, the Khanty lore saved my health.

In the morning, when we woke up in our own shanty, their trail was already cold. Next to the fire lay a new canvas bag and a piece of good rope. And in the fire itself, there were several baked potatoes:

before he had left, the slant-eyed man had been generous to us once more. We felt sad without them, especially without the Khanty.

KAZAKHS

We carried out all their orders, and at midday we came out on the forest path that the man in charge had shown us. The path led us through the forest, almost right up to the reserve tracks. To reach the freight cars, we had to cross a small field. But we were afraid, and decided to wait until dark.

Of the three empty trains, one of them, the longest, consisted of freight cars, platforms, fuel carriers, and several wood carriers loaded with larch logs. This was the one we chose. It was clearly formed to be sent to the Urals. Under the cover of darkness, Mitka and I got into one of the middle freight cars and decided not to sleep – the locomotive might not get put on our train, but on another one. But I couldn't resist, and fell asleep. Mityai shook me, and ordered me to see what was going on – it seemed that we were being detached. And indeed, a third of the wagons, including ours, was being detached from the rest by a small "cuckoo" steam engine, and taken to another track. Our wagon ended up third from the end, if you looked from east to west. We didn't sleep until morning, fearing that we would be taken in the opposite direction, but in the morning, the train suddenly shook – a locomotive arrived from the west and attached itself to our wagons. Three or four minutes later our new train began to move in the direction of Chelyabinsk. Out of happiness at this outcome, we ate two forest-baked potatoes apiece, and slept the sleep of the just.

We spent a day being shaken in our freight car. The train alternately raced or crawled along, or stopped at little half-stations to make way for eastbound trains. The next day, we came to a complete halt at quite a large station, filled with a huge number of slant-eyed swarthy people, who were fantastically dressed in stripy robes, pointy hats and funny short boots. They spoke a gibberish we couldn't understand. In Omsk, these people in robes were called Kazakhs. Could it be that we had come to the Kazakhs?

Like everyone else, they were meeting their demobilized, their surviving children, fathers and relatives. In a vast field behind the loading section of the station, an entire Kazakh camp had been set up, complete with horses, covered wagons and yurts. There was a large bazaar there, where wool, felt, sheepskin, leather, lamb, horsemeat and painted ceramics were sold. The stripy colored gowns, the embroidered felt hats, and the rugs on which the goods were laid out, created a festive mood.

The Kazakhs met the soldiers returning from the front or the hospital as whole families, with children, horses and dogs. They seated them on horses, as heroes, and proudly led them to their camps. We saw how a young man, a completely armless amputee whose chest was covered with awards and medals, was seated on a white horse, a felt Kazakh hat placed on his head, a red-and-white belt tied around his waist, and two elders in striped gowns led the horse by the reins to the bazaar square. In honor of the armless man, people fired hunting rifles, played on unfamiliar instruments and beat drums – evidently the amputee had greatly distinguished himself in the war.

We spent four days among the Kazakhs, sleeping in their yurts. The yurts were laid out on the square, surrounded by carts. The horses were tethered in a circle around the carts at night, with their heads towards the center. The horses served as excellent guards for the camp. The Kazakhs took pity on us when they learned that we were from the north, from Leningrad and Novgorod, and fed us lamb, saying:

"Novgoroda – so far, so far! Leningrada – oh, so far away!"

They wanted me to leave the blind boy with them, as he had an ailment of the lungs, and they would cure it. Mitka refused, hoping that he would soon reach his home, his Novgorod grandmother. To protect his lungs on the road, an important old Kazakh man sewed him a vest out of pieces of sheepskin, and gave me a small piece of sheepskin to sleep on.

On the third day we discovered from the wagon inspectors that our train would leave on the morning of the day after tomorrow, and travel in the direction of Kurgan. This suited us, if only it would not wait at small half-stations for so long. In the morning, saying goodbye to our kind hosts, Mityai and I got into another freight car of our train, and having distributed the numerous gifts among our bags, we had a fine supper of lamb with mare's milk and Kazakh bread. We soon fell asleep. We woke up in the morning – our train was travelling west.

THE CHILDREN OF ARTILLERYMEN

The nights were becoming cold. Mitka was helped by the fur garment he had been given, but still, by morning we were quite frozen. We had to get a woolen blanket from somewhere – at least one for two of us. In Kurgan, where we arrived on the third day, we endured several days, and almost ended up in the clutches of the police again. Initially we worked at the market, but after two days of work, interest in us ran out, and we decided to go to the train station square. A lot of soldiers gathered there, and our repertoire was more suitable for them than for the people at the market, but it was more dangerous, the black and raspberry toadstools could come after us.

Our performances at the square were successful. They kept asking blind Mitka to sing. They examined my wire leaders, passing them around. All the three songs about the leader had been sung, the people asked for more, and Mitka sang a mournful song:

> In the garden by the valley
> A nightingale once sang.
> And I'm a boy in a strange land
> Whom people have forgotten.
> Forgotten, and abandoned
> From an early age.
> I was left an orphan,
> Happiness is not my lot…

He sang about himself, and so well that tears sprang into the eyes of many of the men. When he finished, a big guy in an officers' uniform and a large star on his epaulettes came up to Mitka, picked him up and kissed him to the approval of the others.

As soon as we had finished our performance and started to collect the contributions, two policemen came to our circle from the train station, and asked what was going on. They were told: nothing special – we were singing songs about the leader.

"Where are these boys from and what are they doing here?"

"The boys are ours, children of the division," the guy with the big star on his epaulettes said. "Look at this young boy, who was injured by the fascists. He's with me, on my account."

And he showed them his important identification, and the cops went away.

This was the second time that soldiers had come to our rescue. The man turned out to be an artillery major who had been sent to the Urals with an entire command of subordinates and a special train of railroad platforms for some new automotive cannons. Mityai and I told him about our lives on the railroad, and asked him to help us reach Chelyabinsk, where we would go to an orphanage, spend the winter there, receive medical treatment and study at school. He agreed to take us to the Urals under the condition that at big stations we would not emerge from the wagon.

This time we were very lucky. Chelyabinsk was not far away, and most importantly we wouldn't freeze in empty freight cars. The major fed us a delicious meal at the station restaurant, of borshch, a large meat cutlet with fried potatoes and a real compote of dried fruit. This amazed Mitka and me – we had never eaten at a table spread with a white tablecloth, from white plates with blue stripes around the edges, we had never eaten with such heavy, gleaming spoons and forks, and we didn't even know what it was like to eat with forks. And especially not in a hall with enormous windows, columns, and paintings on the walls. And the waitress – who was so attentive, smiling and efficient – brought us more potatoes than we were supposed to get, and the potatoes fried in oil tasted completely different than they did at the orphanage canteen. After our constant wandering and our half-starved existence, after the dry rations we had eaten, the major organized a well-fed paradise for Mitka and me, that we remembered all our lives.

At the end of the meal, the comrade major took us to the passenger wagon of his train and gave us to a whiskered sergeant major with the order to have us washed, dressed and given places in the upper bunks of the sergeants' compartment. The most difficult thing turned out to be dressing us in clean clothes. Mitka and I together fitted into the smallest soldiers' shirt, and in the uniform breeches we disappeared up to our heads. But what could be done, he told us each to get into a shirt and climb under the blankets on the bunks. He promised to think of something the next day. For the first time in an entire month, we went to bed washed and in clean shirts. In the morning, the sergeant major ran off to the market and exchanged the soldiers' breeches and shirts for children's clothes, which were still too big for us, but not Gulliver-sized.

By the evening, our artillerists' train was connected to a locomotive, and we set off for the Urals, and without stopping.

All the soldiers under the major's command treated us well. We tried not to be a burden on them, and humored them as best we could. Mitka sang to an accordion. He asked if he could try to play it, and the soldiers gave it to him. Soon he was playing it quite well.

"A capable boy," the sergeant major decided. "You'll grow up to be a musician."

For me, they found a twist of thick cooper wire, and I bent it into a large profile of the leader, which the sergeant major attached to the wall of the superior's compartment.

On the third day, we reached Chelyabinsk. The artillerists' train was continuing north, to Tagil or Zlatoust, I don't remember. We didn't go with them. Mitka was coughing heavily, and it was imperative to get him to hospital immediately. And it was also better to spend the winter in a big city. The train stopped on a reserve line, quite a long way from the station. And they started to prepare to transfer to other railway lines, avoiding Chelyabinsk. The major ordered the sergeant major to accompany us to the train station. I don't know how we would have made it to the Urals without the artillerists lead by the major.

He said goodbye to us in the military style, without unnecessary words. He told us to give ourselves up to the police in the city.

THE COP

Before we gave ourselves up to the state, the blind boy and I wrapped the passkeys to the railway wagons in an old piece of tar paper we found and hid them under a prominent house, painted blue, not far from the police station. We hid them safely, placing them on a pillar stone after moving aside the board that covered it. We would take them back in spring. I took the slingshot apart, placing the rubber band in my pants, and attached the tinderbox to my leg. After these preparations, we presented ourselves to the police. To the man on duty I confessed that I had run away from the Omsk orphanage, and that I was headed to my mother in Leningrad. On my journey, I had met the blind boy Mitka on the train – he was with me now. When the weather got cold, he had become tormented by a cough. The doctors should see my friend Mitka. On the road I had been told by Kazakhs that his lungs were in a bad way.

"Comrade policemen, please, help us, send him to the doctor."

I remember that the man in charge, an old war veteran type, growled at us:

"Well then, wolf cubs, you lost a warm roof, it's getting cold and you need some walls until spring, and then you'll run off again, eh?"

We didn't say anything.

We spent the night on benches in the watchman's booth, and in the morning we were sent to the orphanage – an old three-storey building with solid doors. I thought that the Chelyabinsk orphanage guards would beat me for running away from the Chernoluchi orphanage, but I got away unscathed.

CHELYABINSK ORPHANAGE

The boss of the local institution was a tank colonel who was decommissioned because of injuries, and had a face battered by shrapnel. He was an enormous man of fantastic strength, who did not fully realize how strong he was. He looked kind of frightening, but he was kind. His institution was not, thank heavens, a model institution like the previous Siberian one run by Toad. There was discipline, but it was not savage. There was not really any clear internal division into older boys and little kids who obeyed them unquestioningly. There was no humiliation from the instructors either. I can't say that everything was benign. But the people in the Urals are generally harsher and more aloof than people in Siberia. And we boys didn't exactly toe the line at that time, we were like animals that had escaped from their cages.

To start with, according to the rules, Mityai and I were put in an isolation ward for quarantine. After we were washed and clothed in the orphanage uniform, we were fed and taken to the sanitation ward to sleep. The nurses at the Chelyabink orphanage, compared with the monsters in Omsk, were real angels. The elderly nurse, nicknamed Old Pipette, was almost a doctor. The younger nurse, Pipette, was her assistant. They wore clean white gowns, and even smiled. As I later discovered, they treated everyone with drops that they dripped into our noses, eyes and ears. As soon as our throats started hurting, we breathed in the main medicine – a streptocide powder.

Everything would have been fine, but at night Mitya was wracked by a horrible cough that

115

continued until morning. In the morning he was bleeding from the throat. Both the nurses – old and young – ran around in panic. The boss himself, the tank driver, turned up and ordered them to call the hospital. An hour later, medics and a doctor arrived, and took away my blind friend in a car with a red cross on it. As we said farewell, he stroked my face with his hand, and feeling tears, he began to soothe me, saying that he would soon come back to me. Not knowing how these things were done, I clumsily kissed him for the first time. The old nurse pulled me away with difficulty from Mitya, and he was taken away. In desperation, I threw myself at the nurses and started pounding them. I don't remember how I was brought to my senses, but I didn't eat anything for two days.

The nickname of our chief orphanage supervisor, a former frontline officer, was Gold-Mouthed Fang – he had one gold tooth in his mouth sticking out among the other ordinary teeth. Fang held the same position as the Chernoluchi Screwface, but was not as savage, and also his right arm had been maimed on the frontline. When he was in the mood, Fang would tell us about his experiences of scouting out and taking prisoners.

His assistant was Lad-driver, who took us to school, and had also recently been a soldier. He always turned up at work in uniform, only without epaulettes, but with two marks for injuries on his chest.

Besides them, we were ordered about by another two guards, who had clearly been shell-shocked in the war. One was Monofool, the other Multifool. The main occupation of Monofool was lining us up. During most of the free time that wasn't taken up by the school and eating, he arranged us in a line according to height, straightened us, turned us around, turned us back "to the left" and "to the right".

Multifool's favorite expressions were "I don't know", "it's not allowed", and "I have no idea".

Our entire supervising staff was made up of soldiers who had been through the last stages of the war, and for that reason, evidently, they did not treat us so harshly. Even the nicknames they were given were more gentle than the ones given to the Chernoluchi goons. We were fed at the South Urals orphanage much better, or as the local expression had it, richer, than in Siberia. We ate here like decent people, from plates, not out of mugs. True, the plates were made of metal, but they were plates nevertheless. No one took food away from us, not from me at any rate. Additionally, being experienced, during my first days there I made a deck of cards and gave them to the head dude of the orphanage, a big guy nicknamed Sledgehammer. He was stunned – he'd never in his life held such beautiful cards. A little while after that I made another two card decks with a different design, and earned myself his protection for all time. Anyway, the dudes were generally wary of getting up to no good at the orphanage, as the tank driver boss could give any of them concussion with a flick of his fingers.

KNOWLEDGE IS LIGHT,
IGNORANCE IS DARKNESS

The school that I first ended up in could hardly be called an institution of education. It was a long horizontal barracks divided in half. One half painted cobalt green was for civilian, city schoolchildren, and the other, unpainted, of dark brown wood, was for us, the pupils of correctional labor colonies and orphanages of the USSR NKVD. Down the center of the barracks, there was a dark corridor, and on the sides there were classroom-cells. In each classroom, there was an enormous Dutch stove, covered with metal. By the back wall of the classroom, around the stove, there was a tall pile of damp logs. On the opposite wall there was a blackboard made of a piece of plywood painted black. Above the blackboard hung an old slogan covered in flyspecks: "Knowledge is light, ignorance is darkness". Lessons in each classroom took place in three shifts. The city was still filled with evacuees. There was more than enough populace for three shifts at the school – both upstanding pupils and enemies of the people.

In the mornings, when the Lad-driver took us to school, it was freezing in the classroom. The stove tender, Mumuka, a deaf-mute man, did not manage to heat all the classrooms with the damp logs, and we had to help him. After my training at lighting fires with the Khanty, I realized that the split logs should be placed vertically, from the butt-end to the top, like for a night fire. The dimensions of the stoves made this possible. I got it right immediately – the logs burnt much more quickly. Mumuka was very surprised and made me his assistant, and the boys gave me the title of main stove heater.

From the corridor side, on our door an announcement hung: beginner classes. Indeed, in this classroom cell, the first, second and third year pupils studied together. Apart from a few lads, all the pupils in the beginner classes were terribly overgrown. I can't say how old they all were, but many of them had whiskers sprouting under their noses. These children of war were unmanageable. If these big louts didn't like something, they could chuck a log at the teacher. As the stove tender, I sat on the back bench in the central row by the stove, and the split logs literally stuck into my back. My neighbor on the bench was Kunckledragger from the colony. When the teacher called him to the blackboard to answer a question, he would grab a hefty piece of wood out of the log pile and send it sliding across the floor to her, saying,

"That's instead of me, let it answer your question."

When the latest teacher could no longer put up with this outrage and ran into the corridor in tears, a horrible nightmare would ensue in the classroom. The overgrown brawlers jumped up from behind their desks, grabbing the smaller boys, mocking us, "crushing lice" on our heads and tossing us onto the log pile. They turned the desks over, banged logs on them, drew an enormous backside on the blackboard and shouted:

"Hande hoch, hands up – every man for himself!"

It was a total riot. One of the hooligans stood by the light switch and gave us a light show, turning the electricity on and off, shouting:

"Knowledge is light, ignorance is darkness!"

THE HEADMISTRESS
OF THE SCHOOL

This disorder would continue until the door burst open, and the headmistress appeared in the doorway – a grey, short-haired lady in a dark, neat suit and with the gaze of authority. The classroom immediately fell silent. Without any hurry, she would walk to the teacher's desk and with a disdainful tone utter such an incredible tirade against these overgrown hooligans that their jaws gaped in amazement. And furthermore she did not use a single swearword in her reprimanding lecture. But it was invariably strong, vivid, accurate in its descriptions, and always new. For me, a former Pole, these were lessons in the Russian language, and so I listened to her with great interest. The headmistress had such a powerful inner force that she charged the air around her, and all our hooligans and their leader were terribly afraid of her. She gave them such juicy nicknames that all the overgrown louts were at a loss for words when they heard her speak:

"So then, you two-bit barbarians, you've gone and fouled it up again – what do you think this is, Cossacks-and-robbers in your own back yard, you mangy fly-suckers, you stinking gobblers! You want to go on bleating and mooing your whole pathetic lives 'coz you're too cool for school, you meat lice, you pig-snouted slurpers? What about you, you slump-shouldered bum-face, what have you unbuttoned your trap for, you want to knock me over or something? Have a mind to pitch a log at me? Go on, try. You pimpled goon, you're so old it's time you were getting hitched, and here you are still stinking up the second grade. Hear me good and clear – you go and apologize to the teachers for the whole gang this very day, or I'll hand you over to the guards and tell them to unscrew your lustful parts. Got it?! And you, you goatbleating crooks, has the lesson sunk in? I want order in this classroom in one minute, or I'll deal with you fartmorons myself…"

By the end of her royal diatribe, all the louts stood before her in a line, and there wasn't even a peep out of them.

At the orphanage they whispered that in the '20s and '30s she had been christened by crosses, herself, but only for political reasons.

After the headmistress left, the louts put things back in order: they took the small children off the logs, and set the overturned desks upright. For a month or more there was relative calm.

THE LEDGER

The textbooks that I studied from were covered in obscene drawings and swearwords, which meant that I learnt the science of four-letter words from an early age.

For writing notes at lessons and doing homework for all the subjects, I was given an enormous thick ledger for the entire year, in a sturdy cardboard binding which was indestructible. This book was divided into several sections on both sides, corresponding to subjects. On one side I wrote down the lessons, on the other I did the homework. In this great book there was a whole section for drawing, where I drew the card deck kings, queens, jacks and leaders, training for my future life.

In spring, when the school was over and the time came to flee, I gave this treasure to my sidekicks who stayed behind.

GERMAN ALIENS

There was one event at the Chelyabinsk orphanage that I remember in particular. Somewhere around the November holidays, they began to pack us together. Every one of our already crowded wards had two or three more bunks put in it, practically liquidating the passageways. Metal beds were placed in the two wards that had been emptied. The corridor by the exit to the staircase was blocked by a wall covered with plywood, with a door in it. For a long time, we didn't know why such serious preparations were being made. Then rumors began to spread that German prisoners of war, of childhood age, were being sent to our orphanage, like us, only little fascists. I remember that we didn't like these rumors at all. Why were our wards being given to enemies? Why did we, the victors, have to live in cramped conditions?

Indeed, at the end of November, two buses arrived at the checkpoint of the orphanage, and the guards led a whole division of scrawny boys and girls with frightened faces to our floor. We stood in a crowd in the corridor, the whole orphanage, and watched the guards counting off the little fascists, calling their non-Russian surnames. But strangely enough, all of these little Germans spoke excellent Russian. I didn't understand how they had learned to speak Russian so quickly. Even for me, to move from Polish to Russian, I had to pretend to be mute for two years. We started to pester our supervisors, Monofool and Multifool, who explained to us that these little Germans were not Hitler's Germans, but Russians, something like Russian Poles, Russian Finns, Russian Greeks, Russian Jews and other Russian minorities. Their parents had been sent to Kazakhstan when the German troops invaded, and they would soon be sent there too.

We were not mixed with them. They had their own guards, who were more ferocious than ours. The Germans were fed separately from us, and much worse. The entire orphanage was divided in half – one half sympathized with them and even fed them, while the other half humiliated them. If it hadn't been for the guards, they would have been badly beaten. The pimply leader of the hooligans and the bum-faced Sledgehammer even tried to rape a German girl in in the woodshed, snatching her from the group during a walk. The guards saved her when they heard her cries for help, and stopped the would-be rapists in time.

The mighty colonel, the head of the orphanage, held the trial of the perpetrators right in the yard. He took one of them by the collar in his left hand, and the other in his right, raised them off the ground and smashed their foreheads together. After this the concussed boys were treated for a week in the isolation ward by the Pipette nurses, and at the end of treatment they were sent to a labor colony for further correction.

At the start of May, the little Germans were sent away to the East. We crowded around in the corridor and now saw off the Germans as if they were our own . Many of them, saying goodbye, cried for some reason.

THE DEATH OF MITYAI

The first time I was able to see my friend Mityai, whom I missed terribly, was not until the end of November. With enormous difficulty I persuaded the colonel himself to allow one of his subordinates to take me to the hospital for a meeting with my blind friend. When we met, we were happy to see each other. After two months of treatment, he felt better. But I was upset to find out that after he was released from hospital, he would not be sent to us, but to a shelter for blind children, and there he would be taught at a special school. The food at the shelter was much better than at our orphanage, and this is important for lung disease patients.

I was able to arrange the next meeting only at the beginning of March, this time at the special shelter for blind children, named after a certain Ushinsky, where he had been transferred from hospital. I brought him sugar and butter – treats that I had stored up and received in exchange for the cards I had drawn. At first he didn't want to take them. Mityai began to introduce me to his sightless fellow ward mates, as a younger brother. I was only a year younger than him. He felt all right, but looked strangely pale and skinny. We swore to each other that in June we would run away from Chelyabinsk together to our northwestern homeland, and meanwhile we would start preparing for the escape.

The second time, I visited his shelter accompanied by a guard at the end of May. The local old watchman with tobacco-stained handlebar whiskers asked whom we had come to see. I said we were going to my blind brother, Mitka the singer. He knitted his hairy brows, and hoarsely replied:

"Your blind lad gave up the ghost a few days ago, his lungs were full of holes, and that's how it is, my little friend."

I was staggered, I squatted down and could not get up for a long time, or move at all. His death was the first terrible sorrow in my life. I couldn't understand for a long time how I would go on living.

Several days later, the guards handed over to me his sheepskin vest, along with a note written by someone: "For Stepanych for warmth. Your Mityai".

In June, stealing my Khanty bag from the matron, I fled. I fled alone once more, I fled to the west, to my blockade city. To my right leg, I attached a bag with the train keys, the legacy of the Siberian thieves. And in the pockets of my pants, there were once again two measured spools of new copper wire. In the right pocket for the profile of Stalin, in the left for the profile of Lenin. By that time I could already bend them with my eyes closed.

Part 3

CHRISTENED BY CROSSES

Where my mother is – I don't know,
I lost her long ago.
My mother is the thick grass,
My father the wind and the campfire…

(Orphans' song)

ESCAPE AGAIN

With the escape from Chelyabinsk, new patterns in my life in the expanses of the pre-Ural lands among the human taiga began. I ran away from the orphanage by myself, without trying to talk anyone into coming with me, but I ran with the memory and sorrow of the first friend in my life, the blind Mityai. I ran in the May warmth from the window of the school barracks. All of the few clothes I had, along with necessary supplies, had been stored up and hidden in the oven part of the unused old stove in the orphanage. I was able to gather food to last me over three days. The train wagon passkeys had survived the winter in the bottom storey of the old house.

To start with I walked towards the train station, but going around it, went out to the railway tracks and trudged along them to the zone where the freight trains were formed, with the aim of finding a train that was travelling north in the direction of Sverdlovsk or Perm (Molotov). The entire zone turned out to be filled with wagons. It was impossible to find out which trains were going where without asking someone, but I had to ask vaguely, carefully, so they didn't suspect that I was a runaway. My description had probably already been reported at all the main stations. Thanks to the map that hung up at the school, I knew that the end stations in the Chelyabinsk Region were Kyshtym, Mauk and Ufalei. It would be good to get to them as soon as possible. The fact of the matter was that until a runaway leaves the territory of the Chelyabinsk Region, he belongs to it. If I ran away from Chelyabinsk, and reached the Sverdlovsk or Motolov lands, then I would be taken to one of their orphanages – at least this would be further north, closer to Petersburg.

I began to wander between the wagons, in the hope of meeting a suitable person who would help me. And suddenly I saw a dude, five or six years older than me, in a railway uniform cap, and carrying a canister of boiling water, who had clearly been sent from a workers' brigade. Strolling over to him, I asked politely:

"Sir worker, can you tell me where the trains to Sverdlovsk and Molotov are formed?"

"I'm not a sir to you," the dude said indignantly, but he was obviously humored by my address.

"Excuse me, but my grandfather was supposed to come there and give a package to the guard... But I got lost – everything looks the same around here."

"For some people it looks the same, for others it doesn't," the dude said boastfully. "You're in luck: we worked there this morning. Go back the way I came, to the water pump. Between the tracks you'll see a post with drinking taps on it. To the right of the post are the Sverdlovsk trains. Be careful when you walk over the tracks – the wagons jostle..."

In those distant times, at almost all majors stations in Russia, between the tracks, immediately behind the terminal or in front of it, there were drinking posts. In each one of them, in a small niche, there were two water taps – one with cold water, the other with boiling water. At hub stations, these posts were placed for the needs of working people in places where trains were formed. Besides water taps, there was a large metal mug in the niche, which was always attached to the post with a sturdy chain so that customers couldn't take it along with the drink. People came running out of the halted trains to these posts, carrying kettles, decanters, bottles and flasks. Lines of thirsty people often sprang up in front of them. According to unwritten rules, the conductors poured themselves water without having to wait in line.

All the freight cars in the Sverdlovsk train were empty, but they were locked with padlocks, and I reached my shelter on wheels from the other side – through the window, and only thanks to the fact that one of the metal bars of the grill was bent for some reason, and of course thanks to my scrawniness and short stature. But if any officers unlocked the padlock and pulled the door open, there I would be. I wouldn't be able to get back out through the grill in an instant... From such thoughts, I became even thinner. I could only hope that I would be lucky, and pray to God that the train would start moving soon. And soon it did – God helped me. The buffers clanged and yelped, the entire snake of wagons slithered back, and then, after a short time, it jerked forward – and, with the wheels slowly clicking, we were off. I pressed up against a crack in the closed door of the freight car and stared at the passing Chelyabinsk railway structures, semaphores, booths and bridges. Some time after my orphan's meal I fell asleep on some remains of hay that were in the wagon.

In my dream, I saw the blind Mityai traipsing through the wagons of a passenger train with mournful songs:

> In the garden by the valley
> A nightingale once sang.
> And I'm a boy in a strange land
> Whom people have forgotten.

At that time I was gradually turning into a small animal that had escaped from its cage. I felt danger by scent. I woke up at any suspicious rustle or sound. I could tell by scent if I was approaching a house, even people. Bad people smelt in a particular way – badly. In a word, my senses were becoming exceptionally keen.

STATE GOODS

I passed through several stations with names that sounded heavy to my half-Polish ear: Argayash, Bizhelyak, Kyshtym, Mauk and Ufalei, almost without stopping, but with a few adventures.

We stopped to fuel the engine at the village of Kyshytm (a name with my two "y"s, my least favorite letter, the sound "y" in the Russian language took me a long time to learn to pronounce). I made up my mind to carefully crawl out of my den and run for some boiling water, to brew in the kettle given me by the soldiers some tea that I had snitched in Chelyabinsk. Quite soon I succeeded in climbing through the window unnoticed and pulling up the kettle, attached by a rope.

On the way to get the boiling water, as I walked between the cargo trains, I came across an unexpected sight – the railway roadbed and part of the area between the railway tracks from both sides was covered thickly in scattered wheat grain. Flocks of sparrows, jackdaws, rooks and crows were gathered around this unexpected free feast. The sparrows were the most numerous of all. A goods train loaded with grain had probably jerked suddenly or shuddered in this spot, rewarding the train station ground with the precious foodstuff. Upon this bird armada there was slowly backing a string of sturdy prison freight cars with sealed windows, behind whose grills could be seen the closely shaven heads of women, gaping with hungry eyes at the feasting birds. I didn't immediately realize what this train was. I understood from the armed guards standing in the open vestibule of the last wagon.

An entire train of state human goods christened by crosses was moving towards me.

THE CHINESE MAN

The next morning, my train stopped at some kind of hub station. Through the crack, and moreover still half asleep, it was impossible to see anything. But I intuitively sensed something wrong. The mooing of cows could be heard from outside, the stomping of hoofs and the flicking of a whip. I decided to get out of my freight car jail immediately. It turned out that my intuition had not let me down. The entire train, including my freight car, was waiting for a herd of large horned livestock. The station was called Ufalei – the last station, which I had reached by the Chelyabinsk goods train. I would have to get out here anyway. All my edible orphanage supplies had ended, and with the task of obtaining some food somewhere, I set out towards the station.

Noticing the toadstool on the station platform, I decided to walk around it on the village side, and here I came across the local market. At that time, in our villages all the roads led to the market. The half-empty, depressing little bazaar clearly did not have any need for my artistic talents. I had to do something. Hunger is no joke. Maybe I could show the leaders at the canteen, it worked in Siberia, after all. It would be good to find out where the canteen was. The market women in the Urals area were mean and unkind, and it was pointless to ask them, they might even call the cops. When I saw the only man among the saleswoman on the other side of the market, I went over to him. He turned out to be an old, slant-eyed man who resembled a Kazakh. The most interesting thing was that the man was selling painted glass frames for photographs, and pictures with bright floral patterns also drawn on glass. His stall rang out over the entire market square with unexpected contrasts of colors, and radiated some unfamiliar magical energy which stopped me in my tracks and puzzled me. I forgot about my question and literally glued myself to the counter, amazed by this unusual sight. This was so interesting: he was inserting small, wrinkled silver and gold candy wrappers into the bright spots of the flower designs, and surrounding it all with a black outline. I should learn to do this, I thought.

"What are you rooking at, rittle boy, does it rook good?" the man suddenly asked me in a stragely effeminate voice and with an unfamiliar accent. "What do you rike most of all?"

"I like everything. These flowers are very cleverly drawn," I pointed to the glass picture. "I've never seen anything so fantastic before. Where did you get them from?"

"They're Chinese."

"Are you Chinese?"

"Yes, I'm Chinese."

"I've never seen a Chinese person in real life before. I've only seen Mao Zedong, your leader, on pictures and portraits. Uncle, if you could teach me how to draw with paints, ?! I can use India ink – look, here's a deck of cards" – and I took from my jacket a deck of cards that I had drawn at the Chelyabinsk orphanage, and held it out to the Chinese man.

He looked them over, smacking his lips for some reason.

"Velly good, ts, ts... Good, ts, ts... You can't buy card here, ts, ts... Good..."

"Teach me how to paint cards, I'd draw them and paint them – we'd make good money!"

"Who you berong to?"

"No one, I'm running to my mother in Leningrad. I got stuck at orphanages in Siberia and

Chelyabinsk. Teach me, I'll be your helper – your sidekick!"

"Good, good, I have to think… Come tomorrow, we wirr talk…"

"Where?"

"Here, to the market. I talk to my wife Syaska."

"OK, I'll come back tomorrow."

He showed me how to get to the canteen. My trip there turned out largely unsuccessful. My leaders were quite unwanted by the local Chipmunks, as the inhabitants of the Urals are called by their neighbors. I had to exchange my last deck of cards for fodder. I fell asleep on the straw of a freight car forgotten on the reserve lines, and decided to become a pupil of the Chinese man, if he would take me, and stop running until the middle of August.

The next day, with the permission of Syaska, who turned out to be Aska, or rather Anastasia Vasilievna, I was taken on as an assistant by the Chinese artist. The artist, after collecting me from the bazaar with my small bag, took me to his white and blue house, the only painted house on the entire gloomy street not far from the market, and put me in his workshop – a small barn with a window and a working easel by it. There was a painting on it. Under the easel there were boxes with paints, brushes, paper and cardboard. To the left of the entrance there was a table for cutting glass, and opposite it, to the right, there was another table with a kerosene stove for boiling glue and trays for dyeing paper. The storage cot to the right of the door, by the wall, became my bed. The basic training lasted for two weeks, after which the artist entrusted me with stenciling flowers on glass for photograph frames. By the end of June, I was already doing the outline drawings on them myself.

To stop the neighboring Chipmunks from bothering the Chinese man, they gave out that I was Syaska's nephew, who had come from the Vologda area for the school holidays to study his craft. In July, I helped the artist paint the house of a local important person – the director of the market, a Tatar, as it happens. I painted flowers with oils on the glass doors of an old cabinet. In July – early August, Uncle Xiao (this was the Chinese man's name), with my help, made a dozen card decks from stencils. The quality was excellent. The Chinese man got some thick shiny paper from somewhere – a tremendous expense at that time. I had to work hard for him, but he treated me well. Auntie Vasilevna, as I called her, fed me heartily. On days off, which were practically non-existent, the master of the house himself cooked rice; where he got it from, no one knew, not even his wife Syaska. The only thing that was hard initially was that the Chinese man got up with the sun, and went to bed right after sunset. I was forced to change my ways to adapt to him.

The artist was descended from the Manchurians who were hired by the Russian Tsar in the late 19th century to build the Chinese Eastern Railroad. Some of the many thousands of Chinese builders stayed in Russia, and after the railroad was opened they dispersed throughout its expanses. Anastasia Vasilievna was called an "eternal Chinese wife" by the people of Ufalei. This was her second marriage to a Chinese man, the first had died from illness.

Russian women, once they had tried Chinese men, did not want to return to their own.

He taught me a great deal in these three and a half months. The main thing that I learnt from him was the technique of stenciling, which I often used to feed myself in my journeys, "printing" and selling playing cards. He taught me to draw on any surface with aniline mixed with glue: glass, paper, fabric. And to make outline drawings with India ink, oils and varnish. He taught me to use oil paints, and to cover evenly an ordinary piece of paper with anilines of different colors. To work with brushes, add texture with sponges and rags, and many other things.

In mid-August, with the help of the Tatar director of the market, Takhir Adilevich, they bought me a ticket on the Chelyabinsk-Molotov passenger train to Kaurovka station, from where I would make my way north. This was the first time in my life I was going to travel as a gentleman, in a passenger wagon with my own seat. Additionally, for my work as an assistant, auntie Vasilievna gave me small appetizing pies with mushrooms, cabbage and buckwheat.

In the vestibule of the train terminal, on the main wall opposite the entrance, a portrait of Comrade Stalin hung, looking strangely like the Tatar head of the Ufalei market, whose house my teacher and I had painted. In my bag, besides the pies, there were seven decks of most excellent cards, made by me in my "Chinese captivity".

MOLOTOV-PERM

Kaurovka turned out to be a hub station. Here, from my own wagon, I moved to the boiler room of the next train and travelled another four stations on it, then three to four more stations in the vestibule of a second wagon among some workers, then back in the boiler room, until I reached the border of the Perm Region. In this passenger train, I was able to pass a few more stations literally on the footboards of the wagons. But two stations before Yergach, the conductors finally chased me, ticketless, off the train for good

The place where I was thrown out by the state was a rather small village, but nevertheless graced with a river. It was warm August, and I decided to stay there for three or four days, remember the lessons of the Khanty, put up a shanty in a grove above the river, dig a pit for a fire, prepare logs, and most importantly, acquire food supplies by selling one or two decks of cards printed with the Chinese stencil method – the only assets I had. And so I went to the main place here, the shop.

I was not successful in selling the card decks, but a local one-armed amputee with a cunning eye proposed an exchange – two of my card decks for a pile of potatoes, a loaf of bread and a can of fish. Not much, but I had to agree. Outside the shop, a huge dog called Mamai took a liking to me. The men, when they found out that I had been thrown off the train before I got to Yergach, took pity on me and promised to help – a car would be going there for supplies in two or three days, and would also take me.

Mamai liked the entertainment with baked potatoes, and the four-legged "Mongol" stayed with me in my shanty. On the last day of my stay by the river, the dog justified our friendship. In the morning he woke me up with his growling. As I came to, I moved aside the branches of the shanty and saw through the gap that a couple of freeloaders of some sort were snatching the potatoes that had been cooked for breakfast. Our shanty stood above the fire and was screened by a bush, and so they probably didn't immediately notice it. I pushed Mamai forward, telling him to get them. The huge dog threw himself toward the thieves. Terrified, they raced for the river. Emerging from the shanty, I saw a whole gang of tramps looking at us somewhat in fright. Our camp turned out to be on the path of these "wandering minstrels". Just in case, I took my weapon, the slingshot, out my jacket and got ready to take one of their eyes out – I remembered well from Siberia who I was dealing with: these ghouls, this scum didn't recognize anything but force. The weapon was not required. Mamai was down the hill in a flash, and with a powerful leap he knocked over the moron who had been fossicking in the fire, pushing him into the sand with his gigantic paws. The herd of beggars made their escape, leaving their friend to the mercy of fate.

At midday we returned to the village. I was taken in the car as far as Yergach. The parting with Mamai was hard. Over three days we had become firm friends.

In Yergach I decided not to hide from anyone. If I were lucky with the train, I would get to Molotov, where I would give myself up for fostering to the orphanage. If I were caught before I did, I would still be taken there. There was only one night left to travel to Molotov. As it happened, I was lucky. It turned out that the numerous people thronging around the station were waiting for "happy train number 500" – an additional train that had been formed in the Sverdlovsk area out of various old and even suburban wagons. The major part of those desiring to get on the train were evacuated Petersburg families. I joined them, as a person who had also been evacuated from the west.

The train was literally taken by storm when it arrived. As a bit of small fry that ended up in a crowd of people, I was swept into a wagon that had been occupied long before Yergach. The miserable people had plastered themselves through all the corridors, were bursting out into the vestibules, climbing onto the roof, and hanging off the footboards of the wagons. The entire train snake resembled from afar a crawling caterpillar with ants swarming on it. Like a little monkey, I climbed onto the third bunk, and finding a gap under a pipe that divided the compartment, I squeezed myself between crates, boxes and suitcases. Tying myself to the pipe with a belt so that I wouldn't be shifted around by the objects, I lay still. Outside the unwashed windows of the wagon, it was beginning to get dark.

The next day, the "happy number 500" arrived at the ancient city of Perm, which at that time was called Molotov. And a week later I was taken into the local orphanage, to be looked after by the local louts Buttnik and Permopig.

I'm not going to describe my life at the Molotov orphanage in detail. It did not differ much from life in other state institutions. I will just mention a few episodes that stuck in the memory of my head and back.

BUTTNIK AND PERMOPIG

After successfully passing the exam for a lad, in other words enduring the "bicycle", wettie (wet bed) and nudie (when I had all my clothes taken away from me) without any noise or complaints, after a week I went from the isolation ward up a floor to my sidekicks.

There was no warm welcome for me. I was interrogated by a guy with an interesting nickname – Buttnik, or Butthead. He was standing in for the boss. During the war he had served in the anti-desertion forces, which he was terribly proud of. In profile, Buttnik's head resembled a two-sided hammer. His forehead and the back of his head were absolutely identical. The tiny, evil eyes were hidden under his overhanging forehead, and in a dim light they became imperceptible. His flattened syphilitic nose was virtually nonexistent. Someone had punched his lower jaw inwards, and there were moments when his little mouth seemed to be placed directly in his neck.

The first thing, according to their procedure, was to write down all my details. My surname, first name, patronymic, where I was from, where I was going, with whom, why, etc. I told him everything openly, without hiding anything: I has been at the

Chelyabinsk orphanage and had run away to my mother in Petersburg, and on the way I ended up here. I wanted to return home. My mother was called Bronya. But all my openness didn't make much impression on him. Buttnik was interested in my attitude toward the powers in charge, and whether I would agree to help them. He tried to recruit me as a snitch, tempting me with additional rations. I had to pretend to be an idiot, as the criminals taught me in the wild, and inform him that I had a lung ailment and was under psychiatric observation, that I was of a young age and weak mind, and therefore unsuitable for normal matters.

Buttnik was in charge until the middle of December. In December another, real boss was sent to us: a short-haired, wide-nosed, round-eyed short monster, who immediately received the nickname Pig, or Permopig. Indeed, this disgusting skirt chaser completely justified his nickname. In front of everyone, he harassed the teachers, nurses and even the cleaning women, demanding that they cohabit with him. He couldn't care less about us. For him we were just some sort of rubbish. This Oinker got drunk, created debaucheries, burst into our wards at night shouting: "Get up, enemies! On your knees, bitches! Hurry up! I'll show you who's boss, you little fleas! Who ratted on me, you degenerate maggots?! Answer me, you parasites! You'll keep kneeling until morning, until you break!"

Judging from his behavior, he was clearly from the criminals who had gone bitch, who had given important thieves up to the NKVD and as a reward had been given a job at a government department. He became particularly savage, with fists to the mouth and beatings-up, on holidays, or rather after them – at night. We became increasingly brutalized, turning into bitter little animals, making up our minds to do something desperate – to flee from the orphanage, even into the freezing winter.

Intoxicated by the lawlessness at the orphanage, he made a drunken assault in town on the attractive daughter of some NKVD boss, and immediately vanished from view. Our prayers had been heard. Buttnik, for all his faults, was much better.

STREAMING FLAGS

On Thursdays, under Buttnik's supervision, we walked in a line to the railway bathhouse. The other guard could be any other watchman who was working that day at the orphanage.

The red-brick bathhouses, built back in the tsarist times, were not far from us. To reach them, all we had to do was walk down an old street lined with one- and two-story houses with wooden porches, and cross the railway tracks – and there were the bathhouses. On holidays this street, as was proper, was decorated with flags made of bright red cotton.

In 1947, on the eve of Victory Day, they arranged the usual bath for us. The May weather in that area that year was unusually hot and humid. The temperature in the bathhouse turned out to be cooler than outside.

After the wash, the orphanage platoon, back in the blazing heat outdoors, started up our hill. Halfway to the orphanage, the sky above the town suddenly turned dark. We could hear swiftly approaching thunderclaps, and then large drops began to rain down on the festive street. We were lucky, as we found ourselves next to a large porch covered with wooden boards, belonging to an old Perm house. And no sooner did we get to the porch, than there was a terrifying crack. The tree opposite us was spilt open by a bolt of lightning, and all visible space was drenched in a deluge of water. The boys cowered in fear from this unexpected savagery of nature, and covered their heads with their hands, afraid that the porch roof would collapse.

In the darkness of midday, the lightning flashed, rising up the hill – right to the place where our orphanage of the USSR NKVD reigned.

I don't remember how long we stuck around on that porch, glued to each other. But as soon as the downpour began to taper off, the surprised and stunned voice of the little lad Pesky was heard:

"Look, look, what's that… It's pouring red on us…"

We raised our heads – from the two flags decorating the porch on the right and left, a red liquid was pouring onto the ground. The flags hung out on all the houses up and down the street were likewise streaming red liquid. In complete bewilderment, we stared at this mysterious phenomenon, until our head Cerberus Buttkin began to jabber with a certain uneasiness:

"It's running, it's running, the color is running! Damn it, they spared the salt, the bastards!"

Then, noticing our attention and sensing the danger of being witness to such a terrible deed, he shouted at us, ordering:

"Get into double file! Up the street – march! Enemies!"

We ran up the hill, along the street of streaming flags. The rain had stopped, and the sun came out. It shone on our backs.

HER NAME WAS MARIA

My first escape attempt from the Molotov orphanage was a failure. The road to the west only went through Kirov-Vyatka. The devil prompted me to get into a workers' train that was going in that direction. As it turned out, besides workers, railway cops and conductors were also travelling in it. They were going to replace other toadstools who were ending their shifts. They caught me red-handed, and turned me over to the toadstools going back. These cops took the escapee to Molotov and handed him over to the fierce orphanage guards.

Right there in the guard room, they started thrashing the life out of me. I wouldn't be alive today if it weren't for a stroke of luck – one of them turned out to be Belarussian.

In an unconscious state, bidding farewell to this life, I started to pray and cross myself in Polish fashion. The Belorussian yelled at his sidekick:

"Leave him alone, leave him, don't beat him anymore! Look, he's crossing himself, he's saying farewell to this world – that's enough, or we'll offend God…"

"Why doesn't he cross himself the way we do? Huh? Some kind of Muslim…"

"That's enough – or you'll beat him up for good. See, he's praying to God."

The beater took me by the collar and dragged me to the cell, throwing me on a dirty blanket.

I came to from the cold, I was shivering all over. At first I couldn't get up, for a long time I stayed on all fours, then I sat on my left buttock – my right was beaten to a pulp. I crawled over to the brick wall, and tried to get to my feet against it. The freckled guard caught me at it.

"What, you escapee, trying to climb out again, louse …"

In anticipation of more beating I mechanically crossed myself.

"Why are you crossing yourself, you little bastard, in a non-Russian way?" He strode over to me and thrust his big hairy fist at my nose, with the words: "Talk to me, you little sprat, who taught you to cross yourself like that?"

It hurt me to talk because of the beating, but with difficulty I managed to choke out:

"Mother, mother Bronya…"

"Ah… you're not one of us, not Russian…"

Behind the back of the freckled one the Belarussian appeared.

"Leave him alone, don't touch him. He's a Pole. He raved in Polish in his sleep last night, I heard him, and he crossed himself like the Catholics do – with his palm. I know, we had a lot of them in our country, they all cross themselves like that. Leave him alone, he's a weak little guy, you almost beat him to death already! They made Poland into a democracy. Their chairman Bierut came to the Kremlin to pay his respects. See how quickly everything changes! You shouldn't harass the boy any more – you never know what might happen…"

After the beatings and the cold underground cell, I came down with a serious lung ailment and almost croaked. The Belorussian Cerebrus took me to the isolation ward and called the doctor. I was lucky. The doctor was from Leningrad. Her family had been exiled to the Urals back in 1934. She took me to the hospital as a fellow countryman, and looked after me. I remember the hospital as a paradise on earth, and the name of my savior was holy – Maria – the name of the Mother of God.

JAPANAMOTHER

Among the people whom the Molotov orphanage kids respected, and who was considered to be the kindest among us, even though he looked rather cold, was the caretaker Tomas Karlovich, an Estonian devil. This tall, sturdy old man was given the strange nickname of Japanamother by the boys. When I first came to the ward, I heard a lot of strange stories about old Tomas, which initially I did not believe at all.

The old man did not wear shirts, only sweaters with high collars. He could be wearing a jacket, waistcoat or coat – anything, but only over a sweater. The boys said that under this sweater he had fantastic and fabulous tattoos, which made in colored ink by real Japanese "banzais".

There was a legend that he had lived in Japan, in an institution like ours, but for prisoners-of-war.

This combination – an Estonian who had lived in Japan – greatly intrigued me. But I didn't believe the stories about the tattoos – they were trying to make a fool out of me, as a new boy. I even argued with my neighbors at the scoffery and bet a breakfast and supper that they were talking nonsense. But one and a half months later, I lost the bet. The boys weren't putting one over on me. I don't know why, but on one Thursday, Tomas Karlovich himself went to the bathhouse with us along with Buttnik. The boys in my ward jumped on me:

"Well, Shadow, you've lost, now you'll see a real cinema, such a walking museum, like you've never even dreamt about!"

From stories of people who had seen it, I knew what a cinema was, but I had no idea what the mysterious word "museum" meant. And they probably didn't know either – they had heard the teachers and guards saying it about the old caretaker.

In the changing room, we orphans were presented with five tubs, soap and three sponges for everyone. Then we were ordered to undress quickly.

Buttnik bawled at us:

"What are you dawdling for, scum, quick, soap up!"

Old man Tomas appeared in the bath house five minutes later, when the boys, having soaped themselves, jostled around the tubs.

"Well, Shadow, now open your peepers and look, and remember about today's supper…" the boys pushed me.

I didn't hear what they were babbling about. My eyes were fixed on the naked figure of the old man – he was covered from his neck to his ankles with fantastic colored drawings. At first I was even afraid – they moved, with the smallest twist of his body the drawings came to life. On his body some sort of otherworldly warriors in unfamiliar costumes fought each other with swords. Between them were fire-breathing dragons. On his chest there was a large bald man sitting on a throne with folded arms, and in front of him, on all fours, were many little people, also with folded arms. All the groups of pricked-out drawings were separated from each other by a ribbon of clouds. It is impossible to convey in words what I saw on the old man's body. The impression was extreme. I froze. Literally ever centimeter of his body had been worked over.

"Well then, Shadow, how do you like that museum, eh?"

"Just like some kind of cinema, isn't it?"

"Look at his legs – see the trees, with ladies sitting in the leaves, how about that! You hear?"

I didn't hear anything. My eyes devoured everything they saw, and could not tear themselves away.

"What are you staring at, boy, are you frozen to the spot or something, Japanamother? Palych," he turned to Buttnik, "pour a tub of water over him, let him come to."

They poured cold water over me, after which I started to realize where I was. Was it really possible that all of this had been done by people? It wasn't possible, and where could they have come from?!

Many questions sprang up in my mind, but most importantly, I began to dream of learning how to do even a tiny bit of what I was seeing.

I didn't know anything about Tomas Karlovich back then, I found out about him later. During the first Russo-Japanese war, as a soldier in our army, he suffered a contusion and was captured by the Japanese. One day the Japanese camp leaders ordered all the Russian prisoners-of-war to strip naked and stand in a line in front of two banzais. These banzais slowly walked past the naked men, came to a dead halt by the tall, pale-bodied young Estonian man and clucked among themselves, patting various parts of his large body with their child-like hands. Then, after nodding their slant-eyed heads in approval at the naked Tomas, they left the camp. That evening, the Estonian was called to the camp leaders, where through an interpreter, they proposed that he sell the surface of his magnificent body to a famous Japanese tattoo school, for certification projects by its pupils. For this, the school would buy him out of captivity, and, to use our terminology, after the diplomas had been defended on his body, he would be free, and able to cast off from the islands of Japan for his homeland. Tomas, thinking in his youth and inexperience that they would make a few drawings on him like the ones he had seen on Russian soldiers, agreed to the deal. He wanted very much to escape this Martian country as soon as he could, and return from the Japanese world to his own, green Estonian one.

Literally on the next day, he was taken to a school hall, where around a low counter covered with light zinc, many young smiling banzais were sitting. Tomas was ordered to undress. When he was naked, all the Japanese gasped, and rising from their benches, they began to applaud either him – the tall, pale-bodied, broad-shouldered Russian Estonian, or the two banzai curators who had bought him from captivity. Tomas didn't understand who they were applauding, but he felt that he had got himself involved in something very serious.

Every morning, he was taken under guard to this hall, where identical banzai monkeys were sitting on their low benches, and after their head professor had chirped for 10 minutes, the exam session began. Every examinee pricked his composition into the magnificent white skin of the Estonian. Interestingly enough, Tomas did not feel any pain or other unpleasant sensations during these executions. On the contrary, he initially felt euphoric from this tender acupuncture, and even fell asleep. All the examinees worked extremely carefully, cleanly, without unnecessary movements. They didn't bore holes in the skin like our tattooists do, but unhurriedly they inserted thin needles into the pores of the skin, according to the drawing, and injected into them natural ink in an alcohol base – infection was impossible. They didn't snag the blood vessels or pierce the capillaries. One sensed that all the beginning tattoo masters had a brilliant knowledge of the anatomy of the skin.

Time went by. The slant-eyed Japanese graduates of the tattoo school turned Tomas' Estonian body into a large colorful engraving, into a textbook exhibition of the Japanese epic, and a fantastic sight to behold. Leaving the head, neck, wrists and soles untouched, the banzais released the Russian Estonian prisoner-of-war to all four corners. Everything would have been fine, but as soon as he reached the Russian Pacific shore, went to the bathhouse and took his clothes off, a crowd of people threw itself at him, wanting to examine this wonder. They wouldn't let him go, and forced him to show his tattooed body to everyone. He turned into a walking cinema. The Estonian didn't know what to do. He started to wear sweaters and shirts with high collars, and began to wash in secret. Gradually moving toward the Urals, in the Urals he got stuck for good. He never reached Estonia, fearing that he would become the talk of the town, that his bizarre fame would spread through every Estonian village, and that he would become the shame of his old parents. In Molotov, he was taken in by a tender-hearted Perm woman, and he gradually transformed from an Estonian to a Uralian chipmunk. In his old age, he found a job at the orphanage as a caretaker – the boys were harmless for him.

After the "cinema" at the bathhouse, I stuck to him, desiring to learn the art of tattooing. And I was successful. While for all practical purposes he worked for the NKVD, he earned money on the side at thieves' dens by tattooing. He used the Japanese method – with eight good needles – to create subjects from the criminal world at the thieves' order. When he got angry, he cursed – "Japanamother", or more rarely – "Japanese policeman". These expressions were clearly a record in our language of the unsuccessful Russo-Japanese war.

He became my teacher. Thanks to him, I learned to make tattoos by the Japanese method, although it was simplified somewhat. But in the scrapes of life at state institutions, this craft that I learnt from Tomas Karlovich saved me from much adversity, as it was respected in the criminal world.

EMPTY HANDED

I escaped successfully only in my second year at the Molotov orphanage. As I had done originally, according to my old scheme: in a goods wagon. But my goods wagon stopped somewhere on the border with Udmurtia. I succeeded, almost on the move, in jumping onto a passenger train on its way to Izhevsk, and again I hid in the boiler room. Here I passed several stations, before we reached Chepsta. There the conductor noticed me as I left the boiler-room that she had shut. Thank God it happened when the train stopped at a platform, and I escaped her clutches by joining the passengers who were getting out. After struggling through a crowd of people with bags, baskets and suitcases to the end of the platform, I was about to feel safe, when suddenly someone grabbed my wrist. I turned around and saw that holding onto me firmly was a large, pock-marked man of uncertain age – not young and not old, who said to the two other men he was with:

"Look here, what a suitable thieflet. Who are you running from, ruffian? Don't be scared, we won't hurt you. Where did you get the wad from?

In the hurry and confusion of my escape, I had forgotten to hide the train key, and it was sticking incriminatingly out of my right hand, clenched by the pock-marked man.

"Come, let me have this material evidence, lad."

"That's it, I'm done for, what a stroke of bad luck," I thought to myself, for some reason without any fear at all. The guys didn't look like cops, not even plainclothes ones.

"Time to split, or the toadstools will be after you, and we'll all get put in bracelets," the older guy said.

After we had walked some distance away from the station, Pockmark turned to me:

"Let's get acquainted. Where did you run from, Kid, and where are you running to?"

"I'm running from the Chelyabinsk orphanage to my mother in Petersburg."

"Come on, ruffian, stick with us, a nimble boy like you will come in handy in our work."

So, unexpectedly, I found myself first treated kindly, and then tied to a group of train robbers, as a "rubber" boy, one who could squeeze through any crack, not to mention get into the dog box (at that time, many old wagons still had these remnants of the old service). With these three men, each of whom carried a large bag on his back, avoiding the station, we went down to the river, and along its bank we tramped to the edge of a small overgrown village, where we nestled into a solid, out-of-the-way, cabin with all the trappings – a Russian stove, an entryway, a large central chamber with red geraniums. We were met by a kind lady called Vasilisa.

"Meet the new addition, Vasya, at the station we discovered a pioneer holding keys, how about that!

We'll have to take him into the family and teach the boy the burglar's trade."

So, after all my training in various fields, no better off than I had been to start with, I began to learn one of the most dangerous forms of stealing – the train thief.

On three occasions I had to take part in the thieves' trade as a boy who squeezed in through gaps or as a "tap" – a helper in various parts of the USSR on my crooked route home. Three times, I could have been thrown off the train by furious passengers, but God was kind to me. On the other hand, I could hardly have avoided this trade in the course of my illegal, gratuitous six-year journey from Siberia to the west along our railroads, and without any money in my pocket. I won't disclose to you all the events of my service in the burglary business, but I will try to tell about my training and first ordeals in it.

THE SCHOOL OF THE TRAIN THIEF

They taught me, or rather they trained me, like a dog, all three of them. The boss of the gang, Ryty, or Dad, was the most experienced and cunning of them, the second was Permyak and the third, Antip. Evidently I had caught them on "holiday". And for eight to ten hours a day they tormented me. The things they did to me: in the morning, besides all the running, squats and press-ups, they forced me to get into a fetal position many times, and each time they reduced the amount of time required, until they achieved a result of literally one second. Then two of them would take me by the arms and legs, sway me back and forth and throw me off a hill – down the slope. In mid-flight, I was supposed to curl up into a fetal position and smoothly come down, rolling over the grass in a ball. I was taught to transform instantaneously into a spring, and pushing myself away from the step of a porch, jump forwards, curling up into a fetus in mid-flight. They packaged me into an enormous blanket, clapped on my head and tied down a furry winter hat with ear flaps, and beat me with their fists, forcing me to defend myself. The quicker I responded to them with resistance, the better. They wanted to achieve simultaneous, and even better, anticipatory reactions from me. In the end, after numerous bruises, I started to become furious ahead of the blows. They got what they wanted: they developed an instantaneous reaction in me. After this training, for the rest of my subsequent life no one could hit me. I either twisted away quickly, or hit them first. They taught me the close-range thieves' combat, i.e. the techniques of defense and simultaneous disconnection of the attacker at the same time: the opponent thinks that he has already prevailed over me, pushed me against the wall, but suddenly he himself unexpectedly falls to the ground, and temporarily loses consciousness. This ancient thieves' technique – a simultaneous blow with the elbow to the heart and the knuckles to the temple – is called the "elbow" – nature made this distance in a person equivalent to an elbow.

They taught me to use a Finnish knife, to hold it properly, in the thieves' way, and throw it behind my back when the attacker tries to knock it out of my hands. They taught me to trip people up nimbly and unnoticeably, to make a cop or other person tumble over me by seeming to fall, and many other things. They taught me how to pack things ideally, to fold shirts, jackets and pants so that they took up the minimum amount of space in the thieves' pack. They taught me to twist up sheets, towels and linen so that they would preserve their initial appearance after they were untwisted. Most of the packages, including the stolen suitcases thrown off the train, were burnt because they were material evidence, or left in some hiding place – a bush, gutter or ravine. And the contents were collected and rolled up in bags made of sailcloth of a protective khaki color (so as not to attract people's attention), and in this form it was conveyed to "pits" (storage places) or "thieves' kitchens" – into the hands of "legitimate Cains", trusted buyers of stolen goods.

WORK CONDITIONS

The trade of a "train thief" required more than just daily training. Cold-blooded calculation, resourcefulness, keen observation and reconnaissance skills were all indispensable qualities. First, one had to learn the train timetable by heart. In Stalin's time, passenger trains ran meticulously on schedule. They were never late. Secondly, train thieves knew all the geographical nuances of their route: all the bends and turns where the train would slow down, and all the elevations and inclines, where trains also decelerated. They knew exactly when this or that train was going to be passing any of those areas. And they preferred those trains which hit the right "terrain" at night. They carefully watched the passengers board the train, sizing up their luggage and marking the cars they boarded. They targeted two or three travelers as prospective victims. The thieves knew at what time ticket collectors usually checked tickets on any specific route. They never got down to business right after departure. They would let the conductor and the passengers settle in, lie down and go to sleep. Then they would spring into action.

When a thief got on the train, he would first hide in between the cars or in the stoke-room at the end of the train. The thieves had all types of master keys. Once the train pulled out of the station and accelerated, the thief, with necessary pauses, would make his way to the targeted car by walking on car rooftops, so that no one would observe him an extra time. This was called "walking the crocodile spine". Sometimes the "croc-walk" was performed with suitcases. There were no roofed vestibules between train-cars in those days – none of the imitation leather diaphragms they put between train-cars today. With dexterity, it was very easy to instantly climb onto the roof, or in complete darkness to make one's way from car to car along bumpers and suspension hooks while the train moved, having unlocked the end-door on the way.

If a gang of train thieves was exposed, say, on the Kaurovka-Mulianka route between Sverdlovsk and Molotov, they would immediately move to another region, where everything would go as smoothly as before. I recall that they had three what they called "hiding pits" between Molotov and Kirov. One was kept by a lady known as "Cockeyed Matryona," the second by a certain "Speedy Ganka," and the third one, by a woman named simply Froska.

HOW WE WORKED

Before the operation, one of the thieves, Antip, would go on a reconnaissance mission. Antip, who was the least conspicuous of all, would walk through the cars targeted during the boarding to see who was traveling, how much stuff there was, what the conductor was like, and whether there were any cops around. Then someone would go "unseal" the targeted car, which meant unlocking all the doors on both sides, including the two end-doors. The gang leader, who was also the most expert thief, would be the first to enter the car to figure out the best way to grab the stuff. He would skillfully and noiselessly pull out the "corner booty" from under the shelves, or grab stuff from the shelves and set it out in the passageway. Another thief would come along, as if walking by, grab the stuff and carry it in the opposite direction from where the conductor was stationed. The leader would in the meantime "work" the sleepers in the next compartment. If it happened to be the last one targeted, a third thief, the one who would have been keeping watch outside the conductor's door the whole trip, would come and get the last trophies. They all worked with amazing precision. Exactly by the end of the operation, the train would be rolling into a bend or starting to climb, slowing down. The thieves would throw the doors wide open, hurl the suitcases, bags and sacks down the embankment, then jump off the train.

Much later, arranging numbers and shows in a circus, I would often recall my thief buddies. They could all have easily been great jugglers, acrobats, jumpers or tightrope walkers in the arena. In those days, the wooden walls of train cars only came up to the third shelf, and the space above was divided by a metal pipe. I was the "little guy," so I would crawl along the third shelves, easily squeezing myself through between the pipe and the shelf, and push a suitcase down. Another thief would catch the falling suitcase in his arms, without making a sound, and vanish with it from the car. A second thief would come and take me on his shoulders, turning me into a sort of a mobile "crane". Sitting on the shoulders of this "heavy duty" acrobat, I would use both my hands to pull a suitcase out from the third shelf of the next compartment and drop it down. The other thief, who would be back by then, would catch it in mid-air and make off with it in the opposite direction. All of this happened incredibly fast. Without special training, pulling off these tricks would have been impossible. Like circus acting, the job of a train thief required a lot of honing and immense concentration. To a casual observer, there might even seem to be a romantic side to the trade of a traveling thief, but I didn't find that kind of romance very attractive. To make matters worse, Antip began to pester me with all kinds of unwanted endearments. So one day, right before the train was due to arrive in Kirov, I just kind of vanished into the middle distance: I was there one moment, and then I was there no more... It wasn't for nothing they had nicknamed me "Shadow". Enough was enough, as it was I had spent a good three months being herded by those guys. In Kirov, I turned myself in to the government, and was sent to the local orphanage.

NORTHBOUND

There isn't much I can say about the orphanage in Kirov, either good nor bad. It has left in my memory a shapeless gray blur. By the end of my stay there, which would have been next summer, I had made friends with this little fellow named Mumble (or Buba, in Russian) who came from around Arkhangelsk. We ran away together. Buba had earned his nickname on account of mumbling his homework aloud when cramming it. He was a descendant of timber rafters. Why they had been exiled first to Siberia, then to the Urals, Buba couldn't say. His father was killed in action in the Battle of Kursk, fighting in a platoon consisting entirely of GULAG prisoners. His mother with two small children was permitted to return to her hometown, but Buba was for some reason given over to rot in the orphanage in Kirov. Since then, he had dreamed every night of his native Arkhangelsk. He talked me into fleeing north with him, north to Ustiansk Land to the lumberjacks. From there, going through Velsk and Volgoda, I would take off for Petersburg.

As always, we waited for the weather to get warmer before blowing the orphanage. We had stocked a good amount of supplies – dried bread, sugar and salt – in two hiding places. Then, come mid-May, off we split, floated away, vanished.

My experience from previous runs proved useful. We set our course away from the train station, to the sidetracks where northbound freight trains were put together. There was one already in steam, consisting of a few heated workers' cars with chimneys on the roofs, and a lot of flatcars loaded with bridge girders. We couldn't have wished for a better scenario. We had to disappear from town as soon as we could. We walked around to the backside of the train, trying to find an empty heated car we could get in. We couldn't find one. In two of the heated cars, we heard snatches of conversation. Buba put his ear to the wall of the car, and suddenly beamed:

"Can you hear? They're talking like we talk…"

"So? Everybody talks like we talk…"

"No, I mean, like we talk in the north, like my mother talks, like I do… These people are from Arkhangelsk. You want me to talk to them?"

"No, Buba, wait. It's too dangerous. Let's keep lookingfor some place to hide. When we get a good distance away, then you can babble your Arkhangelsk talk all you want. They're aleready looking for us here."

While we talked, the train jerked forward, so we had no choice but to clamber onto a flatcar with girders and duck down behind the wooden frames on which they rested. As soon as we accomplished this, the train jerked again and started inching slowly forward.

The train was moving north, in the direction of a town called Kotlas. Buba and I remained as if frozen for the first two hours, never as much as peeking out. But as evening drew closer it started getting chilly, and the fear of freezing forced us to somehow prepare ourselves for the night. We looked all around the flatcar, but all we could find were lots of pine chips, piles of them. They must have hewed those wooden frames right there in place. We raked all the chips together by the front support. Making a kind of a nest, we got in and leaned against the framework. It guarded us from the wind, but not from the cold. We were so cold we hardly slept that night. We managed to get some sleep in the morning, when the sun came up and warmed us a bit. The train rolled pretty fast, hardly ever stopping. We woke up, had some breakfast and went right back to sleep with the blissful realization that we were now well out of reach of the authorities in Vyatka.

We were woken up by two guys in railroad caps and overalls, asking:

"Who are you? How did you get here? Where are you going?"

The train had stopped at some kind of junction, by a small river. The guys from the workmen's cars were doing their round of inspection to check the cargo , when they found two kids sleeping in some ridiculous woodchip bird's nest underneath the bridge girders. The guys spoke in Arkhangelese, intoning a question at the end of every sentence. With the same intonation, Buba spoke their lingo back to them, reporting that he was born by the River Ustya-Ushya, that he was now on his way to his mother, his sister and his brother, that his dad had been killed at Kursk, that he had no money for a train ticket, that I was his friend, a full orphan, that's why he was going to take me in to live with him in his village, if the guys didn't kick us off the train.

We begged of them to let us ride to Kotlas and then turn us in to the cops, if that was what they had to do by law. Buba said his mother would then come and get us from Bestozhevo, which wasn't too far away.

"So you're from Bestozhevo? Our technician – our second in command – is also from there. He's down by the river catching crawfish. Get out of your digs and go join him!"

The technician turned out to be from Shangala, on the way between Kotlas and Velsk. Bestozhevo was fairly close to the station by local standards – only about sixty kilometres. The Shangala man promised to put in a good word with the engineer in charge for our continued ride.

In the evening, they put us in a third heated car amid some toolboxes and equipment crates. They gave us a few used quilted jackets, a big bowl of hot millet gruel, some tea, and told us to lie low at stations. Buba's countryman announced that once this Northern railway bridge construction team got to Kotlas, it would then be headed farther north to Solvychegodsk, where a railway bridge was under construction. And we needed to go west, so we would have to jump some transport to Shangala or Velsk.

Before the train arrived at Kotlas, the bridge builders gave us some dry rations: millet cereal, tea, sugar and salt. And they let us keep one quilted jacket each. We turned out jackets into body-warmers by cutting off the sleeves, which also made them easier to roll up.

In Kotlas the technician put us on a freight train, convincing the crew, who were also from Arkhangelsk, to give their compatriots a ride at least as far as Uvtiuga. But the night before Uvtiuga, the train was stopped at some small station, and we were told to clear the hell out because NKVD operatives were searching all the trains for some escaped convicts. If they found us, everyone would be in big, big trouble.

"Split in the other direction, there's a cluster of villages about one and a half kilometers away on your right. You can sit this out there."

And that is how Buba and I unexpectedly wound up in these two villages, semi-deserted since the war. The villages were famous for their old people: old man Lampius, rumored to have lived since ancient time, and Paraskeva the Sorceress.

LAMPIUS

The first village, where we spent only one night, was notorious as an "odd" place among the locals. The local collective farm fields there were sown with crops on the days ordered by the local authorities. But private patches were seeded only when the go-ahead was given by Eulampius, whom the locals called Lampius for short, a decrepit old man who spent most of his time in bed on top of his own stove.

Before the spring sowing season, the village folk would drag Lampius off of his stove, wrap him up in a sheepskin fur coat, and carry him out to the porch of his ancestral house. They would sit him down on the bench and ask:

"So, what say you, Lampius? Is it time for us to sow, or not yet?"

Lampius would extract his right arm from the warm recesses of his fur coat, wet his index finger with saliva, and put it out to the wind. He would sit there silently for a minute or two, holding his hand with the moistened finger up in the air. The whole village would fall silent, waiting for the verdict.

"Not yet, my dears, not yet... Wait a little longer," Lampius would say, lowering and hiding his meteorological instrument back inside his coat. They would carry him back in to his stove.

Three or four days later, they would take Eulampius out to the porch again. Again he would wet his finger and lift it up in the air. And then the silence of the village folk standing around would be broken by the long-awaited:

"It's time, my dears, it's time... Go plant..."

Once this highest permission was given, the whole village would go back and start planting crops in their vegetable patches. Half of the collective farm crops would perish, usually because the seeds froze in the ground. But private crops, which were planted later, would thrive and yield a copious harvest, all thanks to the local barometer, Lampius.

PARASKEVA

In the second hamlet, it was ancient Granny Paraskeva who took us under her wing, or "warmed us", as the locals would say, by letting us stay in her big old cabin. The village folk bragged about her:

"Our old crone has a tongue long enough to reach her ear. Listen to her, but don't listen too hard. When she lets it rip, you'll wish you were deaf." We realized this was true when we first met her on the porch of her cabin. She addressed us kids, without so much as a "hello", pointing with her fox's chin at the rivulets babbling all around:

"Look, spring is here! Every little thing is horny, even the sparrows are humping each other…"

Then, without further ado, she declared:

"If anything needs carried or moved, do it yourselves. My legs are no good no more because of my spine condition. I can't stand up. I have to crawl to the outhouse, fill my samovar with a ladle…"

Inside the house, she asked where we'd appeared from and in what direction we were trampling the earth. On learning that our destination was the village of Bestozhevo in the Ustyansk district, she cursed out the local rafters, calling them "unconscionable drunks":

"They feed not off of the earth, but off of the forest. They fell trees, build rafts, and float them down the Ustya to the railway. Back in the Czar days, they tried to get me to marry a guy there, but thank God, it didn't come off. They don't even have collective farms there. Everything is run by some Forest Management… Apart from timber rafting they, Lord have mercy, milk pine-trees, like wood goblins: they gather sap, those savages. When I saw how they torture the poor pines, I beat up my fiancé and fled. If there's one good thing they make, that's their beer, but there's some foul stuff goes into it, too."

From the hall she showed us to the annex, where two empty metal-frame beds stood. She gave us two canvas mattress-cases, telling us to go stuff them up with some hay in the hay barn. When we were done, she said we were invited to come join her for tea in the living room.

Besides us, there turned out to be a tiny baby boy crawling around the floor, wearing a little shirt and no pants, whom Granny Paraskeva called her "descendant". The child was obviously her grandson or great-grandson. Having treated us to some tea, Paraskeva announced that the descendant's mother was due to return from Kotlas that day. She said the boy's mother was a "learned" woman and worked as an accountant for the collective farm.

At the arrival of her daughter or granddaughter with presents for the little crawler, Paraskeva commanded her not to hand them out but to hide them:

"Let him spy out his stuff among the adult stuff and ask to play with it!"

And when her little grandson found a toy and grabbed it without asking, she appealed to us, as witnesses of an outrage, with words of bitter disapproval for the mores of the day:

"Hardly fallen out of his mummy's ass, and already he grabs himself a toy! During my girlhood, such a thing was impossible. Couldn't touch a chunk of wood without asking. Pretending a small log was a doll, even that was by permission. I made me a doll named Mashka from rags when I was seven, but I had to hide her and nurse her in secret. Girls back then... they had nothing coming

169

to them. A girl had three choices: marriage, the monastery, or living in pathetic spinsterhood with her parents. And now, eh? His mother, she gave her love-hole to some soldier who was whistling by. So he whistled this bubble into her. There it is on the floor, panting and grunting, trying to stand up, sick of crawling...

"This is the time when the Antichrist reigns, that's why everything is so askew. All these wars without end, all this merrymaking colored with blood. The men have all been exterminated, that's why the women go crazy. They were all over that whistler, like flies on honey. They danced circles around his privates, they flirted and they giggled. That prick knocked up three of the girls. He reaped quite a harvest, that one. But the village is happy as can be. Forgive me, Paraskeva of Holy Friday, patroness of women, but three little men crawled out of those three to replace the dead ones. Here's one right in front of you, farting away. And the whistler... he planted his seed and flew off like a kite. He never even knew he'd left three sons by three mothers here. The surprising thing is: the 'hollow' girls in this village are jealous of the ones who gave birth ..."

We stayed four days with Granny Paraskeva. We paid our stay with "manly" chores like cleaning up her overgrown yard and her equally neglected well, and stocking firewood for her Russian stove. It was I, of course, who had to be lowered down into the well in a wooden bucket. I scooped lots of grime and all kinds of slimy things out of it. That well had gone twenty years without cleaning. I caught a strong chill while working inside the well, and to keep me from getting sick Paraskeva made me drink some tea with vodka. Thus the home of a village sorceress turned out to be the place where I was first introduced, albeit with medical intentions, to our famous national "cure-all".

On the fifth day, Buba and I once again went traipsing along the rail tracks. We traipsed most of the day. Nothing stopped at our way station. We reached Uvtiuga by nightfall. Everything was quiet by then. We slept in makeshift beds of fir branches and hay under the woodblocks of a snow barrier. The jackets we had got from the bridge builders kept us warm. We hopped a freight train in the morning, bound for Shangaly, the capital of Ustyansk Land. I recall the slogans on the posters in Shangaly, saying something like: "Men and Women of Shangaly! Be Vigilant!" or "Glory of Thy Land Do Keep! As You Sow, So You Shall Reap!"

"DRINK YOUR BEER, WIPE YOUR SNOUT..."

From the station of Shangaly, the capital of Ustyansk Land, to the village of Bestozhevo we covered at least sixty kilometers hiking and hitching any ride we could get: car, tractor or horse-drawn wagon. We had to cross the meandering River Ustya many times on old, worn out ferries.

The few people remaining in the war-depopulated villages we passed lived by timber logging, fishing and growing whatever these northern climes would let them grow. Rough climate, meager soils, and who knows what else, compelled people to come together and form cooperatives. Unlike the well-to-do "chipmunks" in the Urals, these people survived in utter poverty by human kindness alone. Most of the local affairs were run by Lespromkhoz, the timber logging authority. probably for this reason, the living was somewhat easier in the villages of Ustyansk compared to villages controlled by state and collective farms.

The people in the lowlands told us that we would be passing the village of Verkhoputye on our way to the drunken village of Bestozhevo, that Verkhoputye was about to celebrate a religious holiday, and that the village was famous for its fabulous spring, the water from which they used to brew beer for the festival according to an ancient recipe. Verkhoputye was the only remaining place in Russia where beer was brewed in that manner.

Thanks to the local "carriers" (this is what the locals called drivers), our own feet and sheer luck, we hit Verkhoputye right on the eve of their village festival. The village appeared to have been deserted by adults; only some little kids stood there, gaping at us with fear in their eyes.

When we asked where the grownups were, they turned to face the corral and the forest, and just stood there silently for a long time. Only after Buba had shaken the oldest kid back to life did he pull his finger out of his nose, point it at the forest, and mumble, without pronouncing the letter "r":

"Blewing beel in the field."

What kind of nonsense was that? Brewing beer in the field? We followed the kid's finger, crossing the corral and walking into the wood. About a hundred meters later we smelled smoke and heard the familiar crackling of a fire. We followed the smell for another few meters and found ourselves overlooking a large, nearly circular field covered with green grass.

What met our eye there defies description and imagination. At first we were even scared... We thought we had traveled back in time to some folk legend, a fairy tale, an enchanted place, a magic ritual officiated by pagan priests or shamans.

In the middle of the magic circle, resting on three giant stones dug into the ground next to each other a thousand years ago, perhaps by sorcerers or perhaps by nature, stood an enormous wooden barrel, which we initially took to be a cauldron. Steam rose from it towards the gray northern skies. On three sides, from the ground to the tops of the rocks, wooden platforms leaned against the stones. Along the axis of this stone triangle, about eight to ten footsteps in length, a huge birch-wood fire was burning. On its right side was a woodpile of birch logs, on its left was a pyramid of hand-picked, carefully washed cobblestones on a linen sheet. Behind the barrel, heaped up on either side of one of the platforms, were wreaths of dry pea stalks and a stack of sheaves of rye chaff complete with the grain-heads, each tied in the shape of a cross.

On the mouth of the barrel lay a time-weathered plank with a semi-circular aperture in the middle for the plug-stick, which they called "the spike." The spike – an axis, a pivot – was a straight round stick with a sharpened lower end. The spike went through the whole barrel, top to bottom exactly in the middle, securely plugging the drain-hole in the bottom of the barrel.

Finally we realized what they were doing. They were brewing beer with … stones no less. No kidding. They used those same carefully selected round rocks, heated to a "white-hot" condition ("rabbit color", they called it). In the middle of the enormous fire they heated the rocks, then snatched them out with special tongs and raised them along the platforms to the mouth of the barrel. Four people were toiling on the inside of this fascinating architecture. But at a distance of about thirty footsteps, almost at the edge of the field, stood all of the rest of the village populace excluded from the sacred procedure, mostly women with buckets, cans and big bottles in their hands. Officiating over the ritual was a strict-looking bearded old man of about eighty, wearing a festive red blouse with a silk girdle around the waist. The old man, indeed, looked like a shaman or a sorcerer in this setting. Two muscular young men were assisting him. In charge of the fire was an agile invalid-amputee nicknamed Woodleg.

At the beginning of each cycle, the old man put a pea-grass wreath around the spike, then a ryegrass "cross" on top of it, and sank the whole thing in the barrel. His helpers snatched the white-hot boulders from the fire with their tongs, quickly hauled them up to the barrel from two sides and lowered them onto the drowned wreaths of grass. An explosion of steam thrust skyward. When the steam died down, the old man would put another wreath and another rye cross on the spike and sink it in the barrel again, and the boys would fetch another round of white-hot rocks and drop them in. This was repeated until the future beer came to a boil. Then the old man would slow down the tempo of the work, but kept watching to make sure the beer continued to boil. By signs only he knew, the old man could tell if the beer was ready or not. He would lift up the spike with his ritual lever, a knife stuck in the plug-stick, resting on an axe, which lay atop the cover plank, and he would taste the potion. If the shaman thought the beer was not ready, the ritual would be repeated again from the beginning. The barrel would explode, and the steam would rise to the sky...

Only after the third sampling did the beer priest declare the ritual over, and the village stakeholders who had contributed the mash were allowed to approach the "holy of holies". They lined up in front of the drain-chute. Each received a quantity of beer proportionate to the amount of mash contributed.

The head brewer, standing on top of the rocks, would lift and lower the spike with his makeshift lever, and the sun-colored brew would flow down the hollow-log drain-chute into a measuring bucket. The legless invalid, who was in charge of "portion control", blessed every recipient filling a container, men and women alike, with these words:

"Drink your beer, wipe your snout, enjoy yourself in peace!"

It was the fire manager -- Ivanych, an amputee of the last German war -- who put us up. We slept in his empty hut on benches along the wall. He had no family – his wife had died, and in '41 his sons had perished near Moscow. In the morning, in honor of the festival, our host gave us each a glass of the magical beer, but cautioned us not to drink too fast:

"It was brewed strong, brewed for men, and you are still kids."

That ancient brew, devoted to the Sun, was the first beer we tasted. And I have never tasted anything like it again. I recall that, in their pagan potion, besides the familiar taste of malt, hops and water, there were present the flavors of an oak barrel, peas, rye, stones and grass – all the nature of Ustyansk Land, dubbed "Northern Switzerland" by the denizens of the Arkhangelsk Region.

THE CAPITAL OF DRUNKS

We cast off from Verkhoputye for Bestozhevo on the day of the religious festival, hitching a ride with a local guy who drove a sturdy Studebaker. In the village, gaily dressed folk festooned the green hills with their drunken reeling. The driver turned out to be a native of Shangal. He worked for the local Lespromkhoz office, shipping critical supplies – food, medicines, together with mail – from the station to the villages under his employer's jurisdiction. On our way, Buba asked the driver if he had heard of his mother, Pelageya Vasilyevna Ustyanova, who had returned to her home village Bestozhevo about a year and a half ago with Buba's little brother and sister. The guy said he had heard from his shift partner six months before about some woman with children who had returned home to Bestozhevo from exile – only to discover that her ancestral house had been occupied by the village council office. But what happened to her after that, the driver had no idea. Buba became upset. To distract him from his dark thoughts, I asked our guardian angel and driver another question:

"Why do people in these other villages call Bestozhevo the Drunken Capital of Ustyansk Land?"

"This alias goes way back. Years ago, Bestozhevo was rumored to be a wild place where robbers and boozers lived. There was one law for those lumberjacks and timber rafters: a man must either stand upright, or lie down. A man had no right to sit, or he would be branded a slacker. This ditty was then the anthem of the village:

> We drink vodka, also rum.
> Tomorrow through the wide world we'll roam.
> Serve it up, for Lord Christ's sake,
> Or your riding horse we'll take!"

Toward evening we reached Bestozhevo, a scenic village at the river-bend, a pretty large village by local measure. Our kind driver stopped his Studebaker at the main place in Bestozhevo, the shop. The shop turned out to be closed, but there was still a light in the windows. The driver knocked, identified himself, and the door was opened by a pleasant thick-set lady, probably the saleswoman. Six or seven minutes later they both came back out to the porch and he called us.

"Mikhalych, which one of them is Ustyanov?" the saleswoman asked.

"That one, the taller kid."

"My God, what a big boy he has become, and he used to be such a little Kolenka," and she indicated Buba's size as a child with her hand just below her knees. "You mother couldn't wait for you, she's left the village. Your house was requisitioned by the authorities. They had nowhere to live here, and the bosses were afraid to hire her after her exile. She fed herself with day labor – with mushrooms and berries, which she gathered and exchanged for money at the collection point. At first, she and the children settled in with Makarych the bachelor, who let them live in his annex out of kindness , but when she couldn't stand it anymore, she decided to go live with some relatives of your grandmother's in the Nikolsky District of the Vologda Republic. They don't know about her past there, her husband is dead, she might make a decent life yet, and at least the roof over her head belongs to family. She looked for you, she inquired with every authority, she wrote letters, she's still looking. She left her new address with Makarych. She actually left an addressed envelope, so he could let her know if he hears anything about you. And now here you've fallen out of the sky... Mikhalych, take them to bachelor Fyodor Makarych. It's that house – see? – at the edge of the village. You can spend the night there too, and we'll sort out the merchandise in the morning..."

So instead of Buba's ancestral home we ended up in the house of old Makarych. His house was truly ancient – only logs, no sawed lumber-- with a giant Russian adobe stove and a "beautiful corner" where, below a stand holding icons of Christ, the Virgin Mary and St. Nicholas the Miracle-worker hung portraits of Lenin and Stalin, cut out from an "Ogonyok" magazine.

Makarych, when he found out who we were, pulled out from behind the icon a postal envelope with a stamp and Buba's mother's address written on it. He told Buba to make a copy of the address for himself, and put a letter to his mother into the envelope, with the message: "I'm alive and well, ran off to my home in Bestozhevo, I have no money, what do I do next, reply to me, Your Nikolai."

"Got it? Now start scribbling!"

This was bad luck for us. Staying in Bestozhevo made no sense for either one of us. It was better for us to return to Shangaly as soon as we could, and from there for him to go to Vologda to his mother and siblings, and for me to go through Vologda with him -- and on to Petersburg.

Our driver Mikhalych also realized the plight we were in and offered to take us back, but only upon his return from the other villages up north where he had to deliver more supplies.

Early in the morning we helped unload the car, first for the shop, then for the post office. Then we worked at the shop for the rest of the day, sorting and putting away cereals and canned foods, and hauling meat and fish into the cellar. Our well-wisher from the night before, aunt Kapa, paid us with food: sugar, sunflower oil and bread. Food, during that time, in those parts, was considered to be worth much more than money.

For three days we stayed, never leaving, in Makarych's ancient "black" hut (one whose stove has no chimney, forcing the smoke to exit via doorways or windows, or through a hole made for that purpose). For three days we listened to the stories the old Arkhangelsk man had to tell about the everyday life of peasant folk in the embrace of Soviet power.

What he had to say lodged in my memory with a kind of aloofness in the telling, characteristic of a man who had endured much:

"I was born in what they used to call a 'ruddy house'. Nowadays they call it 'smoky house'. It's the same thing – a house with a stove, but without a chimney. They must have called it "ruddy" because it was built with red wood. Red wood is the sturdiest wood. But I don't really know much about this. Never looked into it. See that adobe stove over there? Two families can sleep on it!

"We made a living from agriculture, mainly. But agriculture here never amounted to much… you've seen for yourselves -- slopes everywhere. You wouldn't get very much, in terms of grain, from them. So our parents had to figure out various other trades to feed the family. Take my father, Makar Andreevich. He was a craftsman, lived to the age of eighty-six. What he did was, he rolled felt boots. His grandfather, Yefim Ivanovich, was a wool-carder. We had this grindstone, too, like the kind they have at mills. He used it to grind grains into flour. People came to use his grindstone. My father was also a fur-dresser, he made sheepskins. My uncle Maksim was an accomplished craftsman, who made wood-sledges. That's a sled peasants use to haul logs, hay and firewood. So…

"But many families, including ours, never had enough bread to eat. As I remember, very rarely did we have enough grain to last us from one harvest to the other. Not with this meager soil we have. There was usually a period in summer when we ate nothing but fish.

"We logged wood, too, but only in winter. This was well-organized. We would fell trees and use horses to haul the logs to the river, piling them up on the bank in preparation for the rafting season.

Our rivers take pretty long to settle back into their natural banks after high water, like this year, too. We would have rafts ready by that time. Once the water had dropped, we would send them floating with some raftsmen down the Ushya to the Vaga, and then down the Vaga to the railway. There were whole families who specialized in rafting. There was none of this nonsense like what goes on now, throwing logs into the river and hoping they get there by themselves. We took care of construction-grade wood. It fed us.

"This village also used to plant a lot of turnips. The turnip was a commercial crop. We would plant in the forest, felling some trees to make a glade, burning the shrubbery and then planting turnips. The turnips usually turned out really juicy and tasty, and there was a lot of them. We had all these adages, too, comparing human faculties with the properties of turnips. We would say, "he's as strong as a turnip," or "that girl is so beautiful, buxom like a ripe turnip." This village was a central one, there were four smaller villages adjacent to it. That's why we had two churches – one big, two-story one, and a small one. They were beautiful and very lavishly decorated. The first one – the bigger one – was pulled down in the 1920s. But the small, warm one, the Church of Our Lady of Kazan, survived much longer. Services were performed there on the quiet for a long time, until the bosses of this country ordered all faith shut down and dissolved.

"I was around when they took the bells down from that church and took them away. I didn't see this, but Alyoshka Ushakov told me this guy came by last year and broke the crystal church chandelier with a picket. And so they go on about how he was a good man.

"In 1937 they hauled off our priest, who was poorer than anyone. Our priest was from common folk, with no education at all. They wouldn't have sent some academy-educated priest to a tiny parish like ours. He was taken away by the OGPU, the government secret police.. We all felt sorry, of course, that it was for nothing. What they took him for and why – we don't know…

"Since the village was decapitated, deprived of spiritual purpose, things have really gone downhill. We've turned back to our darkest past. The only entertainment left for the people is to drink the bitter stuff. You know, the earliest settlers in these forests were fugitives from around Moscow, many of them were robbers…"

The old man kept up his Bestozhevo tale of woe until well into the night. Three days later, when Mikhalych the driver came and picked us up in his Studebaker, three lumberjacks stopped our car as we were about to leave the village, and demanded a "hangover tax" from our driver. They sang us a little song by way of a farewell:

> Us they came to beat or kill
> Upon a high hill.
> But they messed with the wrong fellows,
> We use axes for pillows!

YEVDOKIA OF SHANGALY

Upon our arrival in Shangaly, Mikhalych took us into his small house, which was close to the railway station, and let us stay in his attic. His wife, the snub-nosed Dusya, was a remarkably kind woman who was very good at handicrafts. She worked as a seamstress for the only tailor's shop in town. Due to Mikhalych's war injury, they couldn't have children. So they just lived a good, clean life together, the kind of life people have when they are kind to each other. In their tiny town, Buba and I looked like some horrible ragamuffins even in those impoverished times. I had grown out of my pea jacket, which had started to fall apart on me from wear and age. The neighborhood people were curious about where our driver had found such shag-rags and what he was going to do with them. For this reason Mikhalych and Dusya decided right away to somehow get us decently clothed . He gave his army greatcoat – a keepsake from the Nazi War – to his snub-nosed wife, who deftly made it into two cute pea jackets for us, lining them on the inside with pieces of homespun wool donated in our honor by some neighbor women. The jackets turned out so well that Buba and I couldn't believe they had been tailored specially for us. We were hesitant to wear them for a while, not being accustomed to really nice things.

One of Dusya's tailoring clients was this regional Party leader, a very posh and self-important woman with a round Stalin badge on her chest. When this local bigwig saw our two pea jackets, converted from an army coat, hanging in the hallway, she announced with envy in her voice that a couple of orphan guttersnipe didn't deserve such luxury. This woman wasn't from around there, it turned out. She had been sent from the south to run local communist party affairs, and northern kindness was not something she could easily grasp.

One other detail comes back to me. There weren't enough army buttons, the metal ones with stars, for the two jackets, and Buba begged to have them sewn to his – in memory of his war hero father. I didn't object. All I knew about my father was that some military guys had come and taken him somewhere far, far away before I was even born. I wasn't even sure anymore that I was going to find any of my relatives in Petersburg. So the Shangaly seamstress gave me the regular coat buttons taken from our old pea jackets. I actually thought it was better that way, I wouldn't attract as much attention. I still had a long road ahead of me and plenty of time to spend in and out of various institutions before I reached the end of my running.

A few days later, our kind Yevdokia (Dusya) offered me a job helping out with mail sorting in a mail and baggage rail car, which would take me to Konosha, a hub station from where many trains ran south and southwest. Her friend, the mailwoman I was supposed to replace, was taking her sick mother from Shangaly to Arkhangelsk for an operation on that same train. She would not be able to leave her mother's bedside the first part of the trip. No strangers were usually allowed in the mail car, but the head conductor of the train agreed to my presence on account of his employee's predicament, as long as I remained "invisible". I wasn't supposed to stick my nose out of the car at any of the stops. No problem -- my nickname was Shadow, after all. God himself willed me to be invisible.

My buddy would have to stay on in Shangaly until his mother's travel cash arrived. As for me, I couldn't pass up this chance to inch a bit closer to my coveted Petersburg.

By way of farewell, Buba gave me a piece of paper with his grandmother's address in the Nikolsky District near Vologda. Unfortunately, this note was confiscated by the toadstools who searched me at the railway station police office in Vologda. When I asked them to give me back my friend's address, they just barked: "It's not allowed!" What does that mean – not allowed? Who ordered them to come up with rules like those? Who would be so cruel as to deprive human beings of friendship in this cold world? Who would be any the better off for that? From then on, I began to ponder questions like those.

I bade farewell to Buba, Mikhalych and auntie Dusia who had lavished her kindness on us, as though with my own family. I even cried a little.

"HALT, STEAMER! SILENCE, WHEELS!"

Having thanked my travel hosts in advance for helping me along in my life, I cautiously left the Arkhangelsk train at the hub station of Konosha, jingling some pennies in the pocket of my new pea jacket, and carrying a three-day supply of food collected for me by the tenderhearted mailwomen. I descended into the wetness of a never-ending rain, wading through a thick crowd of people protruding from every crevice of every station building that had any kind of roof. My Shadow skills notwithstanding, I could not even dream of infiltrating the station waiting lounge. So I had to hide from the rain under a covered and loaded cart standing patiently by the platform.

Many long-distance trains passed through Konosha, bound for Moscow, Leningrad, Vologda, south, east or west. The Arkhangelsk-Vologda mail train looked the cheapest. It would be good to get on it and erase myself from the Arkhangelsk Region, then turn up in Vologda Land, where I would no longer have to fear: I could even turn myself in, they would still take me to Vologda. The main thing was to avoid the station of Yertsevo. I'd heard that Yertsevo had the toughest inspections – they would check everyone's documents there. A narrow-gauge track ran into Yertsevo, whose other end led to NKVD prison camp land. Yertsevo was the home base of the office that was in charge of the whole wide GULAG world, which reached as far west as Lake Vozhe. There were many escapes in those parts, hence the heightened security. And me, I was a nobody with no papers. They would grab me, beat me up like it was nothing, and, God forbid, send me back to the Arkhangelsk lands. All my labors would have been in vain. I had to hide really well, maybe find some car with a dogbox, I was still small enough to fit in. And I had to acquire a ticket for at least the first two or three station runs. True, at Yertsevo they could arrest me ticket or no ticket, if I had no ID. And where would I get such a thing, who would give me one?

I was sitting there under the cart, waiting out the rain, as those thoughts went through my head. When the rain let up and the crowd little by little dissolved, I talked some young lady into buying me a ticket to the station of Yavenga. Between the mailwomen's pennies and the cash I got from selling my playing cards to some street urchins, I had enough money.

My seat in the car turned out to have been taken. They must have sold their tickets twice, so there were eight or ten "doubles" like me in the wagon. As a small kid, I was told to keep my mouth shut and sit on some sack in the corner to my heart's content, which I did.

Before Yertsevo, I moved to another car just to be on the safe side, and left the train with everyone else at the station, then reentered my ticketed car when the train was about to leave. My innocuous appearance of an average kid saved me. I didn't attract any attention, and passed safely where anyone else would have been stopped. My ticket destination, Yavenga, came and went, but I succeeded in staying on the train for two more station runs by feigning sleep. But the inspector at Vozhega kicked me out, telling me to walk sixteen kilometers back to Yavenga. Yeah, right! Thanks for the good advice, but I was already in Vologda Land.

VOLOGDA TRAIN THIEVES

I decided to stay for a couple of days at this stop, overgrown with firs and pines. Close to the station, by a small stream of the same name, I rigged up a semblance of a Khanty yaranga shanty from fir branches, and was just beginning to gather wood for my fire, when I heard the crackling sound of twigs under human footsteps. Moments later, a pair of big, weathered blokes stood in front of me.

"What the heck are you doing here, kid?"

"Not much… Just putting up a nest, can't you see or something, to catch a little sleep after the road. Are you some kind of cops or something?"

"Aren't you afraid of bears?"

"As if a bear would want me, especially in summer. Bears are none of my business, and I'm none of theirs. People can be worse than bears."

"Where are you running from? And where to?"

"Running far away, from far away. From Siberia to Peter-Leningrad."

"That's quite a run! So how did you wind up here in the north?"

"Pure accident. My buddy got me to travel to Arkhangelsk Land with him, to stay with his mother, but turned out the big shots had taken his mama's house, so she and his siblings had to go stay with their grandmother in Nikolsky District. And me, I'm headed to Petersburg. Hope to find my own mother there, if I'm lucky."

"Looks like you've been through a lot, kid," said the older guy. "That's a great shanty you've built. Been running long?"

"Close to four years…"

"Traveling by rail? Riding the crocs and snakes the whole way?"

"Yeah, rail in summer. But I turn myself in to the orphanage for the winter, to study. What's this, an interrogation? You plainclothes cops, or something?"

"Hey, watch it, buddy! Watch what you're saying to made men, or we'll give you a fir branch beating to remember! Ever cross paths with any train thieves?"

"Yeah, I met some really good ones in the Sverdlovsk Region. Real pros. They covered two regions. I was in training with them for a while, actually. But it isn't my thing. Better I could give you Stalin chest tattoos or draw you some playing cards, if you want."

"Good with your hands, eh? You wanna get to Leningrad or what?"

"I sure do."

"So help us, and you'll soon get there. We need a guy to keep watch. It's hard without a third guy."

So once again they dragged me into this dangerous game. It would be a really close call for me this time, but I would walk. As for them, they got in trouble, and I don't think they ever got out.

"Where are you guys from?" I asked.

"We were staying with his mother here in the neighborhood, and now we found you," the older one replied. "There's a mail train leaving for your Baldmangrad tomorrow night. So get ready, we'll come get you with a ticket to Vologda. Be ready, kid!"

The next day, we met behind a storage shed across from the station, like we had agreed. The younger guy brought a treat from his mother: three plump round cheese rye buns – "shanga" in the local parlance - wrapped in a piece of cloth. After we consumed these tasty goodies, they explained the business to me.

With my ticket, I would go take my place in a car, and just stay "alert" while pretending to nap for about an hour. During the third inter-station run after Vozhega, I would cross into the other car using the doors by then unlocked by the thieves, and there I would hang around the conductor's storeroom, close to the toilet. If I heard anything suspicious inside the storeroom, or if I heard a door opening, I would cough loudly and try to flee back to my car unseen. But if the conductor got me, I would tell him the toilet in my car was busy, and I couldn't wait…

The car I ended up in with my ticket was filled with sailors. I took my side-seat, and then suddenly felt in my bones that things may not go well for my new buddies that night. Not with a train full of big burly drunk guys. If they smelled a rat, they would become ferocious.

My gut feeling was, unfortunately, correct. The next car was also packed with "salty dogs" going on holiday. When I hit that car after Vozhega, I heard all the sounds of a nocturnal "snorechestra". It looked like smooth sailing. In the dark, I first sensed, and then discerned the presence of the older thief in the middle of the car. He gestured for me to stay put by the conductor's lair. The other thief was ostensibly prepared for the "pick-up run" to grab the dislodged "corners." Pressed to the wall, I kept my eyes and ears to the gap in the conductor's door. I heard wheezing and snoring from inside. Suddenly there came a deep voice from way down the car:

"Hold it right there, asshole! Got him!"

There was a stirring sound inside the conductor's room. I began to cough. The conductor's door slid brusquely open. The conductor jumped out and, pushing me towards the toilet, rushed inside the car.

"Jiggers!" the deep voice rumbled. "He cut me!"

Sailors tumbled down from every bunk. I scrammed to my own car, jumping over all the couplings and bumpers on my way. Thank God those doors had been unlocked by the thieves. In my car everyone was asleep. One of the slumberers was calling in his sleep:

"Niush? Niush, where are you?.."

I sank back into my seat. Minutes later, I heard footsteps sprinting on the car roof towards the tail of the train. Following the footsteps there were some gunshots, which woke all the sleepers. Yes, my thief buddies were in big trouble this time. – they'd run into the sailors.

I would have to leave the train at one of the next stations. The whole car was now in an uproar. The rumor was that one thief had been captured, and the other had escaped on the roof of the train and jumped off. The conductor in the next car, the one who had pushed me towards the toilet, might recall some kid who had been hanging out in front of his door, and realize I was the "lookout man".

Train conductors are smart and experienced types. I left that fateful train at Punduga, helping some little old lady down with her bundles.

THE ORPHANAGE
OF CHORAL SINGING

One day later, at Olarevo close to Vologda, there was a police raid, and once again I became a ward of the state, that is, an inmate of the Vologda orphanage for children, which would become my home till next spring.

There was an unexpected nuance about this orphanage in Vologda, which made it different from all the state institutions I had stayed in before. The manager of this home was a contused veteran who had formerly been a musician or a vocalist – a lover of choral singing. The inmates and grownups alike dubbed him "the singing dwarf" for his small stature and his constant humming of revolutionary or communist party songs. On his round little face he wore a Stalin-style moustache which didn't suit him at all, and appeared to be glued on. And if we add his smoking pipe, with which he also conducted music, it becomes clear who the dwarf's idol was. Our little commander wore the predictable trench-coat and riding breeches with high boots – a fashionable uniform for the commanding corps at the time. His noggin was crowned by a giant officer's cap with a red star on a blue band. From under the cap, the mean little eyes of a creepy small dog regarded us. His head injury manifested itself in the periodic scratching of his right forearm with his left hand. Despite this war-inflicted defect, how he loved to conduct music.

But his main organizational and pedagogical talents were focused in the area of choral singing. Our "troops" were formed by the affinity of our voices. Each troop had a sound all its own. Before the Red holidays, or before some panjandrum or inspector came to visit, they would merge us all into an extended choir and made us practice every blessed day for two or three weeks running. The dwarf would personally conduct these phony displays. They would put some kind of crate down for him to stand on, so the singers wouldn't lose sight of him.

The panjandrums would leave us with blissful expressions on their faces, and the dwarf would get honorary citations and carefully hang them up in his office under the portrait of his beloved leader.

Our repertoire consisted mainly of songs about the Great Leader, Comrade Stalin, and his comrades-in-arms, and of other revolutionary and patriotic material. The first thing we did every morning after we got up and made our beds was practice choir singing. Right in our barrack, we would in lieu of our morning exercises sing the latest, freshly minted "Leader" verses such as these:

Stalin and Mao are listening to us.
Moscow-to-Beijing, Moscow-to-Beijing.
Nations advance, they follow our lead
To a better future and unbreakable peace...

Or:

Warmed by Stalin's sun, we stride,
Filled with courage and with pride.
Make way for the cheerful fledglings
Of the Glorious Soviet Land…

During the day, we would learn new revolutionary songs and take singing lessons from visiting instructors. Before supper, we would usually sing three songs to the dwarf's flailing of the pipe: a "Leader" song, a revolutionary song and a military patriotic song. There was no time to study.

I recall another event in which I was the star actor. On the 8th of May, the eve of Victory Day, our extended choir was rehearsing a new series of "Leader" songs in the main room of the institution at ten in the morning. Remembering the year 1945, I made the Leader's silhouette out of copper wire while singing, and it went around from hand to hand. From his vantage point atop a crate, the dwarf spotted that something was not right in the choir ranks. When the song was over, he jumped down from his pedestal and grabbed the wire Leader from one of the kids, screaming at him – quite unexpectedly – at the top of his high-pitched voice:

"Where did you get this, you punk? Who made this? Tell me!"

The kid stood there, silent and frightened.

"Listen, punk, if you don't start talking, I'll keep everyone singing here nonstop till dark! Dinner and supper are cancelled, unless you tell me who made the Leader out of wire!"

I had to come forward. I couldn't imagine that I had done anything wrong. Back in 1945, everyone loved those things. They would admire the handiwork and the likeness of the Leader and give us food.

"I forbid you, you petty criminal, to handle the image of the Leader! Who are you? A no-good derelict, and a son of derelicts! What right did you have to make a likeness of the Leader in wire? Only the honored comrade artists have the privilege of making likenesses of the image of Stalin the Great!"

"But it was in honor of Victory Day…"

"Silence! I'm telling you – don't handle it!"

"But we sing about the Leader all the time…"

"You're going to back-talk me now, you little twat? To the cell, to the cell with him for ten days' detention, immediately! Lock him up right now!!!" the dwarf kept squealing. And the burly security fart plucked me from the ranks by my collar, and dragged me off to the basement. And that was how I chanced to miss the great festival choir show during the fifth anniversary celebration of Victory Day.

I started thinking while in detention: how come it used to be OK to craft likenesses of the Leader before, but now it was taboo? What had happened? What had changed? Was this just the dwarf's private thing, and other potentiates would still allow it? Or could this be the beginning of something completely different?

The Vologda orphanage had this other hallmark, too: the Makarenko Room, where instructors had "talks" with the inmates. On the wall opposite the

195

desk hung a portrait of the "great revolutionary pedophile," gazing down upon his charges with suspicious tenderness in his eyes... It was there, in that orphanage, that I first heard from the older inmates that Makarenko had been a great child molester, as well as a great pedagogue for orphans.

It was the year 1950. I couldn't wait for warmer weather. I'd had enough of playing choirslave, hurting my eyes with the sight of the jerking dwarf. I had started to get ready to leave already in winter: I stenciled a few sets of handmade playing cards. I swapped two of them for a train passkey manufactured by a local technician. I saved up food all May, and finally at the beginning of June I fled this NKVD choir chapel, making for Petersburg, bubbling with hatred for any kind of choir singing, which would stay with me my whole life.

DOWN AND OUT IN CHEREPOVETS

I got to Cherepovets without any trouble, changing a few freighters. Cherepovets is a city of a multitude of smokestacks. I had never seen anything like it, not even in the Urals. That city offered a veritable sneak peek at Hell, the way I've heard rural old ladies describe it during my by then very extensive travels. What was worse, this Hell was positively a-crawl with all manner of security guards and cops, at least it was that way when I visited. People in uniforms and plainclothes swarmed in the freight and luggage area at the station. It was practically impossible to go unnoticed, especially during the season of white nights. I spent two days scouting around, watching how the trains were put together that would run in the direction of Leningrad or the Baltics. On day three, I decided to act. In the darkest time of a white night, I went walking by the trains that had been prepared to go in the direction I wanted. I was moving along past one of the trains, trying to find me a suitable hiding place, when I heard a loud growl, which must have come from the security flykiller who had suddenly appeared behind me:

"Hold it right there, pup! What are you doing?"

Without looking back, I ducked under the car and crawled some distance underneath it on all fours, then ran over to duck under another train, then a third. When I crawled out from under it, I saw a group of soldiers in the dusk, loading some boxes from military jeeps into some solid-looking train wagons. I heard the noises of pursuit behind me, so while the soldiers unloaded a new batch of boxes from the jeeps, I pulled myself up by my hands, rolling into the open belly of the wagon and hiding between some boxes. About twenty seconds later I heard the guy who was after me asking the soldiers outside if they had seen a kid with a bundle on his back, who had just crawled under their wagon.

"Who are you and what are you doing here? You're not allowed to be in the military loading area. Leave the area immediately! We have orders to open fire on strangers!"

"Comrade Lieutenant! Comrade Lieutenant!" a soldier addressed his commander. "What do we do with this character?"

"I'm not some character! I'm a railway security guard!"

"You are under arrest!" the lieutenant cut him short. "You can explain yourself at the commander's office. Now go! I'll follow you."

"Comrade Lieutenant, I was just chasing a runaway kid…"

"Like I said, you'll get a chance to plead your case at the commander's office. My duty is to escort you out of the military loading area and hand you over to the appropriate authorities."

Hmm, they really are after me… The lilliputian killjoy must have alerted every station in the Vologda Region that a minor enemy, yet a dangerous one, had escaped his exemplary institution, and that enemy had to be caught, or everyone would be in big trouble. I was about to thank my unwitting rescuers, when the rollers of the closing car doors creaked, and soon after that came the click-clacking of the buffers on a military train going west.

RIDING THE SHELLS

As my eyes became accustomed to darkness and my head came together enough to grasp the new circumstances in which my life had just landed me, I came to realize with growing clarity that I had progressed from the frying pan right into the fire. First, this was a military train. Second, I was locked in tight and I had no idea when and where they were going to open my wagon. And third, the car was filled with some heavy painted boxes which could contain anything, even mortar shells. I had escaped one danger only to face yet another. And there was absolutely nothing I could do about it.

I had to sleep on the boxes, pressed against the wall. The rows between the stacks of boxes were too narrow. The train ran practically nonstop, so I had no idea what stations we passed. Fortunately, I had in my bundle some bread crusts, an onion I stole at the market in Cherepovets, two baked potatoes from my riverbank fire by the Sheksna in Cherepovets, and a flask of water. This was more than sufficient to make bearable the more than twenty-four hours I was to spend in the custody of this military logistics unit.

A day later, I was woken up early in the morning by the rattling of my door locks. I rolled down off the boxes I'd slept on and sat in front of them, staring at the door, which was being slid open. The soldier opening the door crouched with fear when he saw me, and somewhat stutteringly lisped:

"What…d-do you kn-now! We have a joy-rider!"

After a moment of salience, he asked, sounding surprised:

"How did you get in here, kid?"

Without budging, he turned his head to his right and ordered someone:

"Velimeev, go get the platoon commander! We got a stowaway here!"

And until the lieutenant arrived, tthis soldier never took his eyes off his unexpected discovery.

The lieutenant took me to some building, where the room was packed with top brass: majors, colonels. They questioned me in detail about who

I was, where I came from, and how I got into that wagon. I told them the truth: that I had escaped from the Vologda orphanage and the dwarf, and was trying to go to Petersburg to find my mother Bronya. The flykiller watchman in Cherepovets saw me and thought I might be the fugitive, so he started chasing me. I had to crawl under some trains and eventually climbed into their wagon while the soldiers were busy unloading boxes from their jeeps.

The military guys took me to the mess hall and fed me milk soup and buckwheat gruel. It was there, in the mess hall, that I found out I was near Tappa, Estonia, which surprised and disappointed me no end. The last place I ever dreamed of ending up in was the land of Tomas Karlovich Japanamother. That damn chase in Cherepovets... If it had never happened, I would be in my dear Leningrad-Petersburg by now.

Before turning me over to the regular NKVD, the military men warned me not to brag about riding in a wagon full of mortar shells. If something had gone wrong, there wouldn't be even the ghost of me left.

OLD TYDRUKU

The internal affairs commissioner sent the fugitive with escort to an Estonian orphanage in Tartu instead of Leningrad. The Tartu orphanage was not much different from any other similar government institution. It was cleaner and better organized, but it was also the toughest of all the orphanages I'd stayed in. It was run by a white-bodied, white–haired Estonian communist woman with a commissar attitude. The inmates called her "Old Tydruku," or "Old Girl." In her office she had the two requisite lithographs on the wall above her desk: a portrait of Joseph Stalin on the right, and of Lavrenty Beria on the left. She sounded almost sweet when she interrogated me, speaking Russian with a cute Estonian accent, calling me a "bad boy" – *kuradi poikka* in Estonian – for my repeated escapes. She told me, if I didn't mend my ways, she would place me in a forced labor colony for children – she had the right connections for that:

"It is not far from here... on our Mother River, closer to your Lake Chudskoe."

She would, indeed, place me in that colony, but not until a few months later. Having studied all winter and spring, I was ready to vanish from that sterile institution by the end of May. This curly-haired kid named Ilka (Ilya) wanted to flee with me, except he wanted to run to Riga, not Leningrad. They had just opened a Navy School for young sailors there. One could enroll and become a real "sea wolf" in two or three years. As sailors, we would be completely independent, he said. And I could keep looking for my mom while studying there. And Riga was closer. So I said, OK.

It was all but impossible to flee from that Estonian orphanage, but an opportunity arose by accident. They took a few selected inmates, ourselves included, to a trade school to see what training was on offer, so later on we could pick a trade. The school offered the full ride – dorm accommodation, food, clothes and training. It was an elegant way to remove excessive orphan mouths from the NKVD system.

We disappeared during that excursion. We disappeared by crossing some yard into a side street, then heading west towards the railway. We left town and walked to Ropka station, where we got on a local train to Valga. After a dreary ride, we disembarked at twilight around the 40th kilometer and spent the night on a blanket of fir branches underneath a pile of some railway barriers. We walked another four kilometers in the morning and hopped another train at the forty-fourth kilometer. Only toward evening did we finally get to the station of Valga on the border between Estonia and Latvia.

It was too bad we didn't know that the Estonian-Latvian border divided the town in half, and we didn't know where the borderline was. We thought Valga was entirely in Latvia. We were extremely hungry. Ilka found some pennies in his pockets, all I had was a deck of painted playing cards, but whether anyone here needed them, I didn't know. This was the first time in all these years I had fled without any preparation whatsoever: I had set aside no food, no flask of water, I had no matches and no fuses. These Estonians-Latvians were wary of Ilka and me. Right after I made my first attempt to swap my playing cards at least for some bread outside a bakery, they turned us in. One of the Kurats (the Russian derogatory term for Estonians) had gone and fetched the cops, and we wound up at a police station. And the worst part of it was, the station was on the Estonian side.

A day later, they returned us with a convoy to the Tartu orphanage, where they gave us the proper beating. They threw us in the disciplinary cell for a week. Finally I was summoned to the headmistress's office. Sitting under her leader portraits, Old Tydruku told me that I, such a rotten *kuradi poikka*, would soon be badly missed by the public prosecutor, and that correctional labor would be my shining future.

She was as good as her word. Come September, I found myself in the promised colony by their "Mother River" – the Emaiygi in Estonian – not far from Lake Chudskoe. The colony was housed inside a former Baltic estate, and I would fester there for nearly a year.

THE KOLONTAI COLONY

In olden times, the estate used to belong to a certain German Baron, who had it built like a castle. We were surrounded by mighty walls built from local rock slabs, with round turrets on the corners for the guards with guns, protecting the colonists from the world outside. There were new red-brick guardhouses with stoves and chinmeys at the northern and southern gates. One gate was used to bring inmates in, the other – to take them out. The three stone barns or, more precisely, a cattle-yard, a drying house and a barn with narrow gun-port windows, had been converted to housing for the inmates. Inside each of the barns, three huge Dutch stoves towered right in the middle, but square ones, not circular, and plated with some painted metal. The stoves divided the space into three parts. Rows of two-level wooden bunks extended from the stoves to the door on either side of the central aisle. The boss and the "made thieves" occupied the bunks closest to the stoves. They put me by the door at first, in the coldest part of the barrack, but with time I came into my own as the number one stoker — thanks to my Khanty teacher, I knew how to make wet logs burn. I got promoted and moved to a bottom bunk in the third row, by the central aisle, so I could stay permanently on guard.

It wasn't easy to keep those stoves going. The firewood had to stocked and enough hauled in from the yard for three enormous burners. In winter,the logs first had to be cleared of snow and ice. The ash had to be swept up, taken out and dumped in the ash box. Under observation in the kitchen, I had to chip off enough kindling wood to start the fires. Axes and knives were obviously not allowed in the barracks. I had to get up in the dark, before anyone else, to start the burners in order to get the stoves going by eleven or noon. On days of particularly freezing weather, the stoves had to be stoked again in the evening.

My fellow inmates in this colony were much tougher and harsher than the kids in any of the orphanages. There was rigorous subordination. The criminal hierarchy was clear and iron-clad, as in the infamous Kresty prison:

— the boss;

— made thieves;

— thieves gone bitch (that is, cooperating with administration);

— footmen;

— free men;

— the fags/toilet cleaners.

Everything was like it is in a regular government, albeit under the roof of what used to be a cattle-yard.

Once again, my craft saved me from beatings and humiliations. The fact that I had succeeded in bringing in a deck of playing cards I'd drawn somewhere around Vologda spoke to my great smuggling skills. That deck got into the hands of our cattle-yard boss on the very first day, and he loved it. The next morning, he bragged about it at breakfast to some made guys from the other barns, and told me to prepare two more decks. Thus I became the court artist of the local crime bosses. From card drawing, it's not a far leap to tattoos. And soon my boss was seen sporting a new tattoo on his arm: a grave with a cross and the inscription: "RIP Dear Mother!" It had been done "right" according to all the Japanese rules, using eight needles. No other tattoo in all of Kolontai came close to my work in quality. All of a sudden, there was a long line of people wanting tattoos from me. And I no longer had to haul logs for the fire – my hands were now a valuable asset.

My skill of making wire silhouettes of the Leaders also came in handy in that correctional institution. My boss would extol my craft to his cronies. He would gather a crowd of the uninitiated around, and order me:

"Hey, Shadow-boy, make us a Baldman!"

Or:

"Bend us a Moustache!"

I would do the job while they watched. I was so good at it by then I would make wire Leaders with my eyes closed.

I also worked for the government, painting things. I varnished and painted the furniture manufactured by the colonists. The furniture was intended for internal NKVD use.

I got sick with a cold in December 1951, developing a suspicious cough. Since my file contained a note that I had "weak lungs," they put me in the Kolontai medical unit. On my fourth or fifth day there, the orderly, who was incidentally a village Kurat, woke me up saying someone had come for me. He helped me put my clothes on, led me out of the ward and turned me over to a security guard. The guard checked the list of my "aliases," and told me to walk in front of him to the Kolontai management office, which was in the "Master" building. After crossing the lobby diagonally, we stopped in the hallway by the first door. The guard came to attention and very respectfully knocked on the luxurious paneled door. He was asked to come in, or more accurately, to bring me in. Inside, we found ourselves in the former Baron's study, with dark wood-paneled walls decorated with ornamental paneling. The ceiling was of the same dark wood, coffered with carved roof-beams. I lost myself for a moment in contemplation of all this luxury. Suddenly an imperious voice grated at me:

"What are you staring at, kid? You like what you see?"

I lowered my gaze down from the ceiling to face a military guy I did not know, wearing blue plumage on his epaulets and his cap, which lay on the green felt of the table. A single star ornamented his epaulets. "A major," I thought. "What would a major want with me? I'm nobody to him." The guard behind me saluted and left, leaving me face to face with the humungous dark writing table of baronial provenance, and the tall blue-epualetted guy behind it.

The major sat down at the table, having placed on it a paper folder and, lifting his colorless, glassy eyes upon me, began:

"Last name?"

"Kochergin."

"Given name?"

"Eduard."

"Patronymic?"

"Stepanovich."

"Which of your family members can you recall?"

"My Mama."

"You mean, your mother?"

"Yes."

"Do you remember her name?"

"Mother Bronya."

"Bronislava, right?"

"Yes."

"Who else do you remember?"

"Brother Felya."

"That's Felix, right?"

"Yes."

"Anyone else?"

I was silent. Who else would I remember? My Godfather Janek? My Russian aunts Dunya and Nastya from my childhood? Or my bearded Old Believer priest granddad, who pinched my butt one time and it really hurt? Or my sworn brother Mitka, consumed with tuberculosis? Remembrances of those people quickly went through my head, but I did not name any of them. I knew from experience: the less you tell the pharaohs, the better off you are.

"Why are you silent? You don't remember?"

"I don't."

"Do you remember the surname of Odynets?"

Odynets… What a strange word. Odynets, ogurets, kapets… And there's this letter "y" in it, which I hate so much. The "y" was hard work when I started learning my Russian. No, I did not remember anyone by that name…

"Do you remember your mother's patronymic?"

I tried to think back to my Polish childhood, but my memory did not yield any patronymic for my mother Bronya.

"Do you remember your maternal grandfather? What was his name?"

Somewhat hazily, I recalled a sunny day in spring, a railway station, a train, myself as a tiny tot in my mother's arms. From the steps of the train-car, she was handing me down to some old lady in white, who was calling me Edvas, her grandson. But there were no grandfathers to be seen around us. It was strange enough I could remember anything so vividly from my very early existence.

But what was my Polish grandmother's name? I could not recall… Much later, I would find out from my mother that my grandfather's name was Felix, and his patronymic was Donatovich. My brother, who had died from pneumonia in a mental institution, was named Felix after him. Felix Donatovich, an engineer, was arrested in the "Prom-party Case" in the early 1930s, accused of sabotage and executed by being shot. So he could not have been at that station in Kiev when my mother brought me there, a three-year-old, to show off to her mother, my grandmother Yadviga.

"Do you remember any Polish?" the major man asked. "Can you speak Polish?"

What an unusual question.

"I can probably understand it, but I haven't spoken any Polish since before the war," I replied uncertainly.

But could I really still understand Polish? It had been such a long time. What's he trying to get to? What did I do? What are my mother, my grandmother or my grandfather to him? Is he trying to transfer me somewhere else? Trying to brush up my file?

Suddenly the major rose, grabbed a map case, pulled out some paper and carefully laid it out on the table. Then he gave me a stunning piece of news.

"So, Eduard Kochergin-Odynets, we have found your mother in Leningrad, and we are going to take you to her in a few days."

I just stood there, dumbstruck and petrified by this unexpected verdict, taut as a string in front of him. I had never felt like this before and never knew I could. Then I started shaking, my head swam, and I nearly fell down on the floor.

"Hey, what are you shaking for? Stop!" he yelled.

I stepped back and sank into a chair by the wall. Circles were rolling before my eyes. I couldn't see or understand anything. This could not really be happening! It was too fantastic!

"You got lucky, you got lucky," — went the voice in my head. — "We will take you, we will take you…"

I came to in the grip of the guard, who was dragging me away from the blue epaulets across the lobby of the baronial mansion, back to the medical cell. My cold got the better of me again. I remained delirious for two days, running a fever around 40°C.

Ten days before New Year, they moved me from the medical cell back to the cattle-yard. I was pronounced officially healthy. I had no possessions, naturally, so there was no packing for me to do before leaving Kolontai. The head warden told me my papers would be ready in two weeks, after which they would take me to Leningrad. I had to pay my debts to my "fraternity" before then. The most important job was to finish the Moustache portrait I was doing for Tolya the Wolf, the boss of the middle "barn". I had begun working on that portrait before I got sick. Then I had to print six more decks of playing cards, two for each barn. I really strained myself and hardly slept.

I was clean of all debts when I left to face the new Unknown. Among the memories of myself that I left behind was my portrait of the Father of Nations on the chest of the middle barn boss, Tolya the Wolf, who was, incidentally, a pickpocket par excellence.

URITSKY SQUARE

Our Estonian train rolled into Petersburg
in the dark. My Kolontai warden, nicknamed
Muddy Eye, the composite of a Latvian rifleman
and an Estonian revolutionary, shook me awake
about twenty minutes before arrival. That was just
enough time for ablutions and a ration breakfast.
Half-asleep, I was not yet fully aware what was
happening, or where I was being taken. It wasn't
until the train stopped and our conductor threw
open the car door into the freezing darkness of a
January morning that I realized this was for real.
It looked like my life was about to change. From a
thief, an inmate, a runaway, a hobo and a jailhouse
tattoo artist, I would emerge a regular civilian, as
my Kolontai buddies would have said. In other
words, my life would take a completely different
turn. Muddy Eye, who had brought me there in
order to hand me over to the Leningrad NKVD,
clutched my arm with his bony fingers and dragged
me along the platform and the square towards the
tram stop, never easing up his grip.

"I'll let you go when I deliver you and hand you
over under signature at Uritsky to the Leningrad
bosses and your mother Bronya, as you call her,"
he told me, explaining his unrelenting grip on my
arm.

What he didn't realize was that, in twelve years, I'd seen the inside of so many government institutions and police stations, I had spent so many nights sleeping in the grass or the hay with field mice or rats, I'd ridden all kinds of railway rolling stock, I'd hobnobbed with Kolontai wardens who had the most exotic soubriquets, like Log with Eyes or Stump with Fire, and I'd seen and done God knows what else – so much of it that I'd had enough. And what else he didn't realize was that I was happy they'd found my mother Bronya in Leningrad after her prison term – she had done her time on charges of espionage, Article 58. It would be a piece of cake for me to lose him in the huge crowd at the station or in the packed tram, but I looked forward to my impending unknown freedom. I already had a pretty good idea of what would have become of me in the underworld.

We rode the tram, which was packed with working folk, for a long time, until night became morning. Finally my warden and I descended in the cold blue light onto some amazingly wide street in front of an enormous, wintry park. The outline of a long, barrack-like building loomed behind the trees. It reminded me of the Estonian fortress in which my colony was housed, except this building looked vastly more luxurious and majestic. In the middle of this fortress rose a tall watchtower adorned with pillars. Must have been a watchtower for special guards.

"What's this fortress doing in the middle of a town?" I asked my escort.

"This is the Naval Admiralty. See that spire with a ship?" he said, prodding me along towards the sidewalk.

A short time later we reached the corner of another street, on which trams also ran and crowds of people hurried along on their business. A vast, vacant snowy space arose before my hobo eyes, rimmed by buildings of dazzling magnificence with countless columns. In the middle of this wide field, which was large enough for a whole army of NKVD operatives, rose a tall pillar. On the top of the pillar stood a dark, winged angel-dude with a cross in his hands. "What's up with that?" – I mused as I crossed a large street on a green light for the first time in my life. What's a church angel doing up on high in this star-studded country?

Behind the pillar there stretched a palace-house, column after column. And on its roof stood ranks of costumed prison guards, like the guards on watchtowers guarding the perimeter of a labor colony. We started walking on the right side of this giant parade ground, along the high yellow wall of a circular house, which must have been built in ancient time for some giant-size warriors. Muddy Eye immediately straightened up, came to attention and started marching, jerking me out of my gaping stupor. When he referred to the house we were walking by as Main Headquarters, anguish washed over me: would I really once more have to plead my case before cops or even a prosecutor, explaining my countless escapes from orphanages and colonies, at this headquarters of theirs? And I felt a chill go through me inside my worn-out state issue pea jacket in the middle of this giant depopulated plaza, hemmed in on every side by the palatial homes of leaders and prosecutors.

We, street kids, believed that prosecutors were the most important bosses above all men, like

215

kings, except kings had gone into the past with the fairy tales, but prosecutors were real. They called them "palace-keepers" in the crime world. Was this name given on account of these palaces of theirs, in which they ruled?

Muddy Eye had his claws wedged deep into my right wrist the whole endless trip. Walking by a enormous arch, artfully linking two identical semicircular buildings, I spotted the huge molded ornaments on the walls. Weapons, suits of armor, helmets… I was particularly impressed by the gigantic, overbearing sizes of all this. But for some reason it came to mind that those would make some good tattoo drawings for my criminal clientele. Behind the arch, in front of a huge door with an NKVD coat-of-arms, the Kurat finally let my arm go, in order to pull my file out from his leather briefcase. The door proved so heavy he had to put his briefcase down on the snow and use both his hands to open it. Behind the first door there was another, guarded by two identical NKVD bullies in spic-and-span uniforms with identical faces and People's Commissariat moustaches, as if made with the same stencil. My warden inexplicably took his Estonian-Latvian hat off, smoothed his rarified locks, and handed them my file. The guards poked around in it for a while, then let us behind the barrier and pointed to a solid oak door. Behind the door, we entered a roomy hall that reminded me somehow of the numerous police stations I had been to between Siberia and Estonia, only this one was much bigger, cleaner and more posh. "Great! They're finally going to do me in here!" – I thought as I entered this headquarters of the pharaoh-Gulliver cops. But nothing alarming happened at first. They told me to sit down on an oak sofa left of the front door, closer to the window. That was a lucky break – I ended up sitting next to a big, hot radiator – on the way I had frozen myself solid. Having warmed up a bit, I began eyeing this NKVD digs. A massive oak barrier divided the room with the lofty ceiling into two parts: one for the cops, the other for the regular folks. There were two doors on my, public side, and two more on the cop side. All the walls were faced with oak panels taller than me. Massive oak sofas stood by the walls and in between the windows, looking exactly like the kinds of sofas they had in railway stations. Only these had the NKVD sword and shield emblazoned on their backrests instead of the Railway Ministry's "MPS."

In the cop area, at the desk by the barrier sat the captain on duty – the master for a day of the front room of the cop headquarters. But the first thing that caught my eye in this hall built for giants were two portraits facing each other. Between the two windows overlooking the plaza hung a portrait of the Leader in a white tunic with the Generalissimo star under his collar, and the familiar cheerful conspiratorial squint of a murderer. That was the richest portrait I had ever seen. It must have been done by some professional painter, a top-notch one. I actually rose and approached it to take a closer look at the workmanship. Noticing my interest, the officer on duty said with a tinge of pride:

"Nicely done, eh? Positively lifelike!"

I concurred. If only he knew what a great job I had done tattooing portraits of the Moustachioed One for five crime bosses! Two on the forearm and three on the chest. One of the thieves had intimated

217

to me that Moustache was "one of us" – a made criminal, christened with crosses, who had done time more than once. Where were they now, those thieves I had tattooed with likenesses of the Leader for protection?

Behind the back of the smoothly ironed captain hung a portrait of the "Goatee" – Felix Emundovich Dzerzhinsky – the same size as the portrait of the Leader. Looking at him, I recalled one New Year's Eve, when I was a little kid at the NKVD orphanage in Omsk during the war, how I appealed to the Founder of the Secret Police in Polish (I still spoke Polish then) in the room where the decorated tree stood and his portrait hung, asking him to give me back my mother Bronya and my older brother Felya or Felix, his name-sake. In return, I swore by the Mother of God that I would mend my ways and become an exemplary inmate. But he had not been receptive.

The day-master of the headquarters frontroom took his time checking my file of papers. Sometimes he would ask something of my warden, who stood behind the barrier on the public side. Eventually he rose from his desk with one of the papers in his hand and made for the door. "Must be going for a seal of the cop-prosecutor, the lord of all the Kolontais of the USSR," I thought. "Needs to seal a waybill for me. Needs to let my escort go back to Estonia."

"Kaikki, Poikka!" Muddy Eye suddenly said with a wink. "That's it, boy!" (Estonian). "Soon you'll be a local kid, a Leningrad kid."

He came up to me and clapped me on the shoulder, seeming kind for the first time.

"When are they going to bring my mother?" I asked.

"They'll give you directions on how to live your life, then they'll bring her. Don't worry. This is it! You're free!"

But as soon as the captain appeared in the doorframe, my Estonian well-wisher morphed back into a Latvian rifleman. He took the paper from the captain, put it in his briefcase, clicked his heels military style, made a sharp left turn and exited the room without saying goodbye or getting to see with his Muddy Eye my mother Bronya.

The captain's admonition turned out short and sweet. He told me, once I was out, never to tell anyone where I had been or where my mother had been, otherwise we would both find ourselves in big, big trouble, and we would never be able to escape them. He wrote something on some paper and gave it to a cop private who was rushing around door to door. The captain rose, leaning on the barrier, and motioned towards the opening door, unexpectedly saying:

"Your mother's here."

From behind the giant oaken door to the right of the Moustache portrait there emerged a lady, very thin and very beautiful, with a cap of wheat-colored hair styled likea wreath around her head. She cautiously approached me across the room, walking against the light. She looked at me with large, surprised grey-blue eyes. She was saying something, but I couldn't understand a word. I recognized her language, I used to speak it when I was a child, but I had forgotten it… I felt confused. I rose from the heraldic sofa, hid my hands behind my back for some unknown reason, and just stood there, petrified.

"Stop with your Polish nonsense! Speak the language to him! He speaks Russian now!" the neat captain told my mother. He was observing the scene from behind the oaken barrier.

"Listen to this cop bullshitting my mother! What a jerk!" — I thought as I came to.

She gave a shudder and stopped in front of him, as if trying to recall something. Then, straightening her wheat-colored hair, she suddenly addressed him politely in the familiar tongue:

"How about some ID for my boy, comrade officer?"

The guy choked and answered meanly:

"I'm no comrade officer, I'm comrade captain. You'll get all the appropriate papers…"

Comrades, comrades… everyone's a comrade here. I remembered a city with a strange-sounding Mongolian Horde name of Kui-By-Shev, where at the beginning of the war I had been summoned to the mental institution to be questioned by a doctor. My brother Felya was already an inmate there. Along an endless hallway with barred windows, two mustached orderlies, looking like composites of all our Leaders at the same time, were dragging across the floor this tiny wrinkled old man with a beard, and he was screaming at the top of his high-pitched voice:

"Are you people or are you comrades?!"

And every time he screamed, they would shake him like a rag, and then keep dragging him along…

When my papers were ready and we were free to leave the cop headquarters, I once again directed my gaze at the Leader portraits, and I thought that the Iron Felix had given me back my mother, after all, but he didn't save Felya. Felya had died of pneumonia in the mental institution of that very city, Kuibyshev, in the winter of 1942.

I do not remember the details of how we left the domain of the pharaohs. All I remember is, we started walking across the giant snow-covered Uritsky Square diagonally towards the central pillar with the angel-dude and the frozen palace of the Tsars with its dancing columns and iced-over sentinels on the roof.

My mother and I, without discussing it, walked very quickly, probably we both wanted to get as far away as possible, as fast as we could, from the NKVD grounds. We did not slow down until we reached the foundation of the angel pillar. I looked back for the first time. From a distance, the Main Headquarters Arch looked like the "dress" tunic of a chief military prosecutor from a film or a dream, beautifully embroidered with embossed symbols of war and violence. Instead of a cap, overhanging the uniform were six black horses with two drivers on the sides. The horses pulled a black dray with some winged lady inside, holding the "double-headed chicken" in her hand. "What kind of weird film is on here, in this USSR? This lady on some primitive cop prowler, could she be a symbol of prosecutorial power? And those other two winged creatures with wreaths on the arch, blessing the swords and the axes. This is screwed up!"

While I marveled at those wonders, my mother had gone ahead towards the Admiralty fortress. I caught up to her and I heard her muttering something in her gentle tongue, muttering to herself. But what -- I couldn't figure out. Later I understood. She was walking and praying to her dear Polish gods.

The tram stop was located right across from the Admiralty. Apart from a bundled-up old lady with a mutt in her arms, we were the only people at the stop. A tram pulled up. We got in the second car. Not counting the conductor, the car was empty. It must have been specially for us that the conductor lady announced the next stop: the Exchange. I asked my mother if we had far to go.

"Your birthplace is only five stops away," she said, smiling, softening all the hard sounds in her words.

Through a peephole provided by a miniature thaw in the ice-cloak of the window, I saw the white, ice-covered Neva River for the first time since I had last been in Petersburg twelve years before. I saw another giant bridge right across from us, and the Peter and Paul Fortress on the left. I had never seen such vast expanses inside cities anywhere, from my orphanhood Siberia to my ex-con Estonia. It was a strange first impression: this vast space made my ears hum. Mother was saying something to me in Russian, but I was shaken by all I was seeing, unable to conprehend. The only thing I remember said in that frozen, empty tramcar is:

"Be careful, son, don't tell anyone what happened to us. In this country, it is easier to plant a man behind bars than to plant a tree in the ground."

I remembered the captain's admonition, and felt a chill go through me again.

My Petrograd homeland proved more welcoming, familiar and forgiving than the oppressive, peremptory city center. Not all the houses had been rebuilt after the war. There were still noticeable traces of the bombings, but normal people walked the streets, and some of them actually smiled at me and my mother. A red-headed woman with a storybook name – Yadviga – answered the door on the third floor of an old house at Ropshinskaya street. When she saw me, she started muttering something in her own language, often repeating: "Matka Bosca! Matka Bosca! Mother of God! Mother of God!"

I was in a large clean room with two windows and a white-tiled fireplace-stove in the corner. It was warm from the heated stove. An oval table laid for dinner stood underneath an old lamp with three winged boys, holding three candlesticks each. Amid the simple white tableware towered an antique candlestick with a candle. In the right-hand corner, as in peasant huts, hung a likeness of the unfamiliar to me Virgin Mary, which Yadviga called Matka Bosca of Chenstokhov. A bouquet of some large beautiful rushes stood in a tall dark vase on the corner table underneath it. The women called these rushes "palms" for some reason. Behind a tall, wide dresser a bed was hidden and, across from it, by the opposite wall stood an ottoman, covered with a pretty, green, red and black stripy wool runner. In between the windows stood a bookcase with antique books and a bust of some Polish poet. What I saw looked so unusual to me that I would remember the scene for the rest of my life. I had seen something like that in films, but only rarely, since most of the films they had shown us were about the revolution or the war. This was my aunt Yadviga's room. The flat belonging to my mother and me on the fourth floor had been requisitioned by the "prosecutors" when everyone in my family went to prison. We were now guests of these Polish people in Petersburg until we found our own housing.

"Dzien dobry! Good day!" said a tall old man as he came into the room – my Godfather Janek. While my mother and aunt Yadviga bustled about in the kitchen, uncle Janek told me how I had used to travel under the tables in his studio.

It was a fabulous dinner. My Godfather Janek lit the candle and raised his glass to "Amnesty" – at least that's how I interpreted what he said. I missed half of what they said in Polish, everything was mixed up in my head. I wasn't yet quite sure which world I was in. But I sensed some kind of awkwardness between me and my mother. We were collaborators in misfortune. We were eyeing each other with caution. She probably needed more time, too, to realize this was all for real.

I passed out right at the table. A hard day combined with lots of delicious food – pelmeni in beet stock and lentils with carrots – finally got the better of me. Mother laid me down on the ottoman and I immediately plunged into an abyss. I could not tell how long I had been falling. I remember finding myself back in Uritsky Square, at the entrance of the Main Headquarters, from where the two twin cop bullies are kicking me with Mother Bronya out into a snow bank. We get up and run cross the frozen square towards the trams and the fortress with the spire and the ship on top. When we reach the middle of the vast plaza, by the pillar with the winged dude, we hear some noise behind us. We turn around and see that we are being chased. A whole army of giant cops wearing ancient armor, red stars on the crowns of their hats, armed with swords, spears, axes and shields from the walls of the Main Headquarters Arch, is advancing upon us. Up ahead, atop a high granite pillar soars the captain on duty, huge black wings stretched behind his back and black sword in hand. He yells loudly at my mother:

"Stop with your Polish! Speak the Language to him!..."

We quicken our step.

Again I look back in fear – and from high atop the arch right upon us the six black horses descend, harnessed into an ancient dray, driven by a fish-eyed prosecutor. And from the walls of the palace the innumerable columns detach themselves and together with their lamps start gathering around us, pressing us in. We run as fast as we can along the narrow corridor still remaining free, toward the beckoning golden ship of salvation. And suddenly the captain from on high gives the order:

"Halt! Or I shoot!"

And then all the icy prison guards atop the royal palace turn to us, lift up their rifles and click their gun-bolts.

I fall to my knees in the snow and, crossing myself with my palm, scream:

"Matka Bosca! Matka Bosca! Save me and spare me!"

Then I awoke in horror and perspiration. I was shaking all over. Mother Bronya was standing over me, telling me in Polish:

"Co z tobą, mój drogi synku? Co ty krzyczysz? Wszystko będzie dobrze. Jesteś jedynym meżczyzną w rodzie, i powinieneś żyć[7]."

---

7 What's wrong, my darling son? What are you screaming about? Everything is going to be all right. You are the only man left in the family. You have to live! (Polish).